M000012242

Planting Wolves

Neda Disney

Copyright © 2019 Neda Disney

All rights reserved. This book or any portion thereof may not be reproduced or used in any manner whatsoever without the express written permission of the publisher except for the use of brief quotations in a book review.

Printed by TANDEM Books, Inc., in the United States of America.

First printing, 2019.

ISBN: 978-1-7333524-0-6

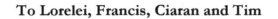

To Lorelei, Francis, Ciaran and Tim

"Boo, Forever

Spinning like a ghost
on the bottom of a
top,
I'm haunted by all
the space that I
will live without
you."

— Richard Brautigan

ACKNOWLEDGEMENTS

Great thanks to Elizabeth Weinberg, Tim Disney, the Disney, Hauser, Loughman, Lord families, my father and mother, RPDFF, CalArts, REDCAT, Charlie Fink, Bill Haney, Suzanne Warren, Alessandro Camon, Mari-An Ceo, the Pourang family, the Karkairan family, Berni Fried, Scott Silva, Aimee Mann, Ryan O Roy, Luna, Local 705, Nanda Dyssou, Max Martini, George Paaswell, Vernon Scott, Brian Dannelly, Vanessa Marshall, Matt Sweesy, Kenny Hillman, Honey Dubrovsky, Kenda Greenwood Moran, Nick Griffin, Berit and Nicholas Edelson, Darcie Shields, Sarah Graham Hayes, DFW, WNYC, Living Now, French Church, Lack Of Dilemma, Pathfinders, Moorpark and all of Bill and Lois's friends.

Table of Contents

• CHAPTER ONE •

The Writer
1

• CHAPTER TWO •

Mrs. Randall
51

• CHAPTER THREE •

Rodney
115

• CHAPTER FOUR •

The Sponsor
152

• CHAPTER FIVE •

The Sex Addict
189

• CHAPTER SIX •

Nelly
197

• Chapter One •

The Writer

HE HAD FINALLY SETTLED on an Armenian dentist near the university and made himself go have the crown looked at. At this point, it had the appearance of a Chiclet but was conspicuously a different sort of white than the rest of his teeth. Its cracked candy shell couldn't even be called a different sort of white. It affected how he smiled; he used his top lip as a kind of hood and tilted his head downward. It affected his awareness of himself when he spoke, and he was pretty sure that he had developed a certain rapid-speech style intended to shorten the time the tooth was exposed and visible.

But it was the legacy of his biological mother, since it was the thing he had apparently come to his adoptive parents with, a smashed tooth. And even though it was a baby tooth that had been broken, the gum had been damaged, so his adult tooth had not come out right, either.

The thing had grown out gray, and once he'd been old enough, his parents had sent him to get a crown. The bum tooth had been whittled down and a veneer popped over it—one that had felt strange and creamy and didn't match his other teeth, so it made him just as uncomfortable as the gray stump under it. But the crown had eventually turned gray, too. Everything wanted to turn gray in his mouth.

The whole thing was a reminder of some event that had happened to him in his first home with his first parents—some event he didn't recall but that had left him with this souvenir bit that had tagged along in his mouth for much of his lifetime.

It was time to go change it and possibly look into having some sort of titanium stake put into the bone so that a stylishly well-matched fake tooth could be screwed in permanently and planted once and for all in his mouth. He thought about how on TV when the police wanted to identify a nameless and decomposed or messed-up body they would look at dental records. He found this rather chilling, but at the same time, it made getting dental X-rays feel sort of pressing. So, as he sat waiting to have his teeth X-rayed, he felt a vague reassurance coupled with a certain disquiet that he would be identified should he end up in some sort of fiery situation where all but his teeth would be rendered unidentifiable.

In the waiting room, sitting across from the writer was a man who looked very familiar. His skin was tight and tan but also sort of pale underneath the tan. His nose was turned ever so slightly up at the tip, although it didn't seem like it should have been, as though it had been convinced to do this against its better judgment. The guy's hair also seemed to be not necessarily as it had wanted to be but forced into place in a certain way. The overall look of the man was attractive but alien.

He was sitting in the waiting room with that awareness some pretty girls have, knowing that they are being watched. A knowing that comes with practiced peripheral sensitivity and the experience that someone was always looking at them. And that knowing and vigilance sometimes follows the person even when they are not being watched, even when they are alone. Eventually, it becomes a magnet, forcing eyes toward them simply by the vibrating energy that comes off them: the energy of the stalked eventually mimicking that of the stalker.

So the writer found himself staring at the man in the waiting room, simply because his subtle movements were strangely loud and designed for an audience. And before the writer could regain his manners and look away, the man looked back at him. His eyes were a sparkly blue, and they were the realest yet most out-of-place thing about him.

The writer realized instantly that the guy was someone he'd seen on television. He wasn't sure what program, but he felt uncomfortable for having stared at him and gave him an awkward, apologetic smile. In return, the guy nodded as if to say, "Don't worry, I'm used to it," then returned an even wider smile, which made the writer stare all over again, because the guy's teeth were the whitest things he had ever seen. He was indeed a television guy. Not even a guy: an actor.

Then the actor spoke, and the writer thought someone had turned on a radio or a TV. He did not at first register that the voice had emanated from the actor. It sounded as if it was entirely manufactured on a soundstage. The writer had never heard anyone with such a voice speaking normally. It was as if the actor could throw his voice across the room, or as if this were the voice of some screen icon from decades ago that had been interpreted and reinterpreted. Just hearing such a voice in person seemed impossibly strange.

The writer felt that perhaps he had never even considered the wonders and potential of a person's speaking voice and was saddened by his own collegiate drawl. But he had to speak, he had to be polite and answer the question the actor had asked him about why he was there, so he breathed in and tried to generate a great voice of his own as he replied, "I'm here, umm, I'm here to get some X-rays and maybe get a little—to have a crown removed and replaced with an implant, maybe."

The actor acted as if he had just heard something extremely interesting.

"Oh, yeah, man, I've been down that road before! I really suggest implants. Don't even go down the whole crown or whatever or bridge road, though, man. Just have 'em screw in some implants pronto."

"Yeah, that's what people tell me. That's what I've heard."

The writer looked around awkwardly, unsure of what to do next, so he simply settled his gaze on the actor, who didn't mind being the place eyes landed when uncertain about where to go.

The actor was wearing a leather vest over a denim jacket over a gray Harley-Davidson T-shirt, along with slightly ripped jeans and incredibly polished Doc Martens. In response to the writer's gaze, he made a big show of looking down at himself and saying in a poor reenactment of nonchalance, with a sudden folksy accent:

"I see you lookin' at my clothes. Yeah, I been ridin' my motorcycle. I take my bike to a shop nearby, and we ride from here once a year. It's for charity, and thousands of bikers ride from Glendale to LA. I realized today I'm going to be here a day early and have a few hours to kill, so I had my assistant make me an appointment to get my teeth cleaned—you know, bleached. They do this laser thing, and, oh my God! In one hour your teeth come out looking like snow!"

The writer could not believe what was happening. He could not believe the things the actor was telling him, and in total earnestness. The writer hadn't been in Los Angeles very long, so he didn't know that this was normal conversation.

He felt like he was talking to a cartoon, and he didn't know what to do. He knew that the actor seemed normal when he was in front of a camera and translated through many, many layers of separation between himself and the audience. He knew that the actor appeared normal once he arrived in your living room through the television. But in person and without any of those borders and boundaries, he was a complete and utter freak.

It was as if the actor's ability to talk to an ordinary person in a waiting room had been corrupted to the point where it could only be infomercial-esque. Every act of relating to others had, in essence, been corrupted for him.

He seemed unable to stay in the present moment. His need to anticipate what the other person was thinking or how they might react to what he said drove him to a sort of distraction as he engaged in a kind of micro–time travel, moving forward by increments of a second to gauge what might be said, and backward by equal amounts of time to analyze the last utterance for clues about the very near future. His fellow conversationalist was both the camera and his audience, with a slight delay between them in which the actor operated.

In this case, his audience was the writer sitting across from him, someone who by his very profession could not help but notice, break down, and seek to identify what it was that made the actor so weird.

The writer could see that talking to the actor was a rare opportunity to observe someone with very unusual instincts. Someone who responded to unseen cues and inner workings no one else was cognizant of. Something about the actor's fame and standing in his profession of being seen and judged may have made him able to function on such a highly predictive level. But most likely he was that way from birth and had simply found a calling that put his euphoric paranoia to use.

Before he could initiate more experimental conversation, the writer heard his name called right after the actor had predicted that his name was about to be called—the actor had made sure to mention it before it happened, and sure enough, he was right. He had kept one eye on the receptionist, considering the rhythm of her movements and breathing in conjunction with who had been waiting the longest, and he was able to sense her impending call to the next patient and to voice his prediction before the event.

And so the writer stood up and said, "Good luck with your ride and teeth bleaching," and then walked through the frosted glass door to the other side. He realized as he walked away that the actor was not so much an actor as a re-actor. He reacted to everything around him, and he was so good that one could easily mistake him for a psychic.

It was an amazing encounter, and the writer felt incredibly fortunate to have witnessed someone like that. He knew it would be difficult to write him as a character, because no one would believe such a person could exist. He also knew that he would have to write him as a joke or comic relief because he could not bring himself to delve into the seriousness of the matter. He could not even begin to imagine the loneliness and fear that must have been there for such a personality to sprout up in self-protection. Yes, if he were to honestly recount such a character on paper, he would somehow break his own heart.

*

It was during a visit to New York City for a book signing and reading that he had truly understood the huge sadness. It was like a thing he had always suspected was there but had never been able to really name.

Then he'd come face-to-face with it.

It happened like this. Some good people from the corporate flagship of a national bookstore had enthusiastically invited him to a big megaplex store and advertised for months for his reading and signing, and had paid for the fancy hotel where he would be staying in New York. These people, these good people, respectful and kind in the extreme, were willing to pay for whatever he wanted and even sent someone to pick him up from the airport. An efficient young girl.

She had met him at the airport and driven him to his hotel, and she had gushed so much over him that he had been grateful she was not in any way sexually interesting to him. She was like a student he might have had in his creative writing class—chubby, glasses, very excited about the functions and uses of her brain.

She'd probably never been in a place like Los Angeles, where all the spirit and sense of beauty would have been sucked out of her instantly, where her mind would have become obsolete, where currencies such as cleverness were not recognized or used for the purchase of anything. No, she'd had the chubby, smart role in all the right places, in New York and Chicago, and in other Midwestern cities.

He could tell this by her confidence. He could tell that she had no idea (or perhaps simply did not care) how she appeared. If she was not the "It Girl," she simply did not mind. Her youth was all that she needed, for now. She was excited, not just about him, but about her whole life, about being employed by the bookstore franchise and being given the opportunity to pick up writers from the airport, to take them wherever they needed to go, to be at their beck and call, picking up their favorite crackers so they could eat them within the safety of their hotel rooms and all kinds of other things.

He could tell how important this was to her, and it hadn't been about the task or the job itself. The experience was somehow giving her hope, which she would take into her life as a kind of nourishment. It would carry her forward to other tasks and other things. It was as if while living the day at hand she was also looking into a crystal ball and seeing how wonderful everything was going to be.

Something about this girl made him sad. Something about her strange, naive confidence. He felt the need to apologize to her relentlessly. "I am so sorry for being late and so sorry you have to do this. You really don't need to do that. Oh, so good of you to come get me." A feeling of embarrassment went into high gear around her. She really was just a girl, not a woman or a child. She was truly and definitely a girl, and everything about her defined girlhood in age, stature, and experience.

The writer found himself silently apologizing for what he feared would happen to her in her life. As they walked down to catch a cab to the book signing, he found himself apologizing for the man that she would end up with, the pretentious, lazy grad student with floppy hair who would trap her soft farm body in the city and who would hypnotize her with talk of John Updike and Norman Mailer until her youth was completely gone.

He didn't know why he was thinking like that. She was probably having a perfectly great life and would fall in love and have adventures and a good career, maybe read a few books, then have some kids. Why was he projecting such misery onto her young being? That's when he realized that perhaps it was him. Perhaps everything he wrote, everything he thought up, and everything he was, was darkness, and because this darkness was who he was, this was all he saw.

And the fact that he'd awakened to this realization intellectually didn't help him find the exit from that state of being.

They got to the bookstore early. It was on Union Square. He could see its massive window displays from the park. He decided to sit alone on a bench at the edge of the park rather than go into the store early with the girl. He said he'd be right in. Instead, he watched the line of people who were there to buy his books and have them signed form around the building. They had come to gaze at him and listen to him read from his latest book and a little bit from the older classics, too.

He simply couldn't believe it. He watched them and noticed how none of them recognized him when they glanced the short distance over and saw him across from where they were waiting. He was not in the proper context. He felt slightly sad about this, as if without his book he was nobody, as if, in a sense, he was his own book's "plus one" guest.

He studied a couple who were especially tall and handsome and interesting-looking, their clothes tailored in that downtown New York way that you'd never see anywhere else, and they were speaking to each other gently. They were sharing something funny. They were attractive without really striving to be, simply by virtue of the places they shopped and the area where they lived. This had made them accidentally chic.

They spoke quietly. Even though they were too

far for him to hear what they were saying, he could tell by the effortless, mute movements of their mouths that what they were saying was hushed.

They were looking at each other, into one another's eyes, and when one spoke the other listened and nodded, and then when the other spoke the first listened and nodded, waiting gently. Even waiting a little after the other had finished a sentence before speaking, not jumping right in to reply or take the next turn.

He watched them, and even though he could tell they were not having a romantic conversation, he saw the love pass between them. They were probably just talking about the asparagus they had for lunch or what they wanted to do for Christmas or even the way somebody they knew had had his hair cut. The intimacy with which they exchanged their thoughts with one another and gazed steadily while the other spoke pierced the writer's heart.

He looked around and saw New York, saw everyone in it, from the unfashionable falafel guy to the kids to the beauties strutting with designer bags—all of it. There were just too many people of too many varieties, too many shapes and sizes, too many stations, all of whom overwhelmed him and troubled his desire for safety. Isolation was the only way to reduce how many different moving parts there were in the world, because the more moving parts, the more chance there was of him seeing or hearing something that would break his heart.

It could be anything. Even while sitting on the bench and turning away from the couple to repair his wound, he would be looking in another direction. Perhaps he would notice someone put their foot up on the low, black, painted metal fence that surrounded the flower beds of the park, see them place their foot on the fence or maybe on a hydrant to tie their loosened shoelaces. Maybe he'd glimpse that private moment between the person and their shoe and watch them have an experience not available to anyone but themselves. He'd watch as they put their foot back on the ground and head toward home or work or wherever it was that they went, that he would never know about, and his heart would hurt again.

He just wanted to understand why everything made him so sad. He put his head in his hands and peered down at the ground. He saw the tossed gum that had turned black and made the sidewalk spotted, something everyone always told you about in big cities: "See those dark spots on the sidewalk? Those are all from pieces of chewed gum people have spat on the ground." And they'd tsk, tsk.

The writer marveled at all the DNA that could be extracted from all the gum spots in some far forensic future. Thousands of years later, all the black spots would help some distant, white-smocked descendants figure out if millions of ancient New Yorkers had had a cold or worse and what mutations and what genetic strengths were most prevalent among the gum-chewers of 16th and Broadway.

And, of course, this made him sad about the fact that he did not chew gum. His teeth were sensitive, and sometimes when he looked at them, they appeared vaguely wooden to him. Did he come from a family of men with bad skin and bad teeth but very good hair? Tall, athletic men who had the wrong types of brains for athletic bodies. Men with depressive, math-oriented brains. There was something strange about looking like a quarterback and sounding like a scientist. A mathlete. But he supposed it came in handy. He never got his ass kicked. But, boy, did he ever get his feelings hurt.

Dusk was coming on, and he was in New York, alone. He knew that his little concierge-helper-girl was probably fluttering around, wondering if he needed something, excited that the reading was about to start and in some way feeling like she owned him a little because she'd taken care of him, as people do when they take care of people. They begin to own them a bit and maybe even feel saddened when the person they took care of recovers and finds his own way again.

The writer sat on the bench and thought about how it would be to go inside the bookstore and how he would feel all the bonds people had with him. He'd look at the love people were about to pour on him and know that love would never get inside him. Because he was not able to participate in it, because it was one-sided adoration without the intimacy required to transform it into real love, the kind that could be shared. And so he knew he would feel lonelier than ever.

He stood up from the bench, fixed his shirt a little, took a deep breath, and went toward the entrance. He walked without looking in either direction, knowing peripherally that he was safe from collisions with pedestrians. He headed to the giant bookstore and, as he came closer, straightened his shoulders and looked at the people in line.

One by one, they began to recognize him, and one by one, their faces went from intense thought to startled smiles. At first, his demeanor was solemn, but then he smiled back and nodded. This made them feel like they shared a secret with the writer, confirming that, somehow, somewhere, in someone's bedroom, living room, hotel room, classroom, they had been close to him.

The writer and the reader had shared a moment where they had understood one another completely, right down to their bared souls, except that the writer had not been there. Only his words had, only the thoughts that he had had two years prior to the reader's discovering them. Like gazing at a star that twinkles long after its own death, the reader had seen only the writer's emanation and had loved it, even though there was nothing there and the reader had also been alone in a room, just as the writer had been when he had recorded his long-expired thoughts.

The concierge-helper-girl saw him approach and reached out her arms as if to embrace him but quickly lowered them and finally dropped them to her sides. She would never fully know the correct welcome and erred on the side of stiff giddiness. The writer helped her out by gently taking her rigid arm as if to do-si-do and escorted her into the megaplex. The people in line saw this and chuckled, the girl blushed and committed the writer's kind gesture to the treasured memories of her youth, and for one crucial moment, the cold and distant light years melted between all of them.

*

The bartender was an attractive woman, which he could tell was going to make things easier. So, after waiting long enough for it to seem casual, he asked her where he was. She smiled at him, as if partly not understanding him and partly getting what he was trying to say but either not knowing the answer or not wanting to give it to him. So, ignoring the question, she asked if he wanted another whiskey.

"Sure," he said. The thing was, he could drink. He could drink and get the perfect sort of buzz that he hadn't had in years and not worry about his medication because he felt really great. There was no depression, and it didn't feel like that medicated state that was just keeping depression away.

There was just nothing, no underlying anything. He felt like he did when he was young, and the drinks hit him like Slurpees. They gave him a quick buzz that went away.

This was good. This was not going to be a sloppy bar experience. No, it was fine. He let go of the fear and tried to figure out what he was supposed to do next, as in a game, and then he would do it.

Really, he thought, he was a smart guy, and this sort of thing was easy to predict. His mother would simply walk in the door, red hair flowing, in some sort of indescribable dress, and smoke like before they knew it would kill you, and the whole thing would unravel, and it would be amazing.

"Well," he said to the bartender, "I'm here to meet someone."

"Oh, really? A date?" she asked.

"Well, sort of."

He felt a little uneasy at how pleased he was with the bartender's assumption that he was waiting for a date and how comfortable he was with the idea of waiting for a date with his own mother. But, you know, she was only his birth mother. She hadn't raised him, so the mother/son thing had never really developed between them, and if the bar was on some other plane of existence, as it clearly wasn't Earth, then perhaps she would come in as a young woman, and perhaps all laws would be suspended, and perhaps now he could date his mother.

Freud had made the whole issue of dating your mom a little commonplace and hardly a special secret anymore. Besides, what he wanted was a date with a mysterious redhead from the '50s—not his real-time parent in mom jeans. He started to laugh. It was good to be smart. Sometimes he really understood how good it was to be smart. To not be baffled by your own inner workings and your own humanity and the way your psychology had developed. How it balked and folded like an accordion playing itself.

Self-knowledge was good. It was good to know what was happening and not always be a victim of the unknown. He felt an immense gratitude for his intelligence about the Freudian moment and looked up from his drink and back at the bartender, who was smiling at him and watching him.

He wondered if she was smart or if her personal life was one big mystery to her as if her own personality were an unknown and she just stumbled around, and things simply happened.

She looked at him and, as if hearing his thoughts, answered, "It used to be like that for me but not anymore."

The hair on the back of his neck stood up.

He thought, "What the fuck? Did she just read my mind?"

He stared at her, wondering if she'd read his mind again, and it seemed that she had.

"You'll get used to it. Most of the time, I'm not

all that interested in what people are thinking, but seeing as you're new and it's the beginning parts where you're not quite sure what's happening, I'm paying a little attention. But yeah, you can have private thoughts about pervy stuff with your mom if you want. I have my own stuff to think about."

She nodded at the other side of the bar, and it was as if the man sitting there had reappeared after having been there before but somehow fading away, just her motioning to him made him come back into definition.

She said to the man, "His thoughts are so loud and crazy. I didn't have a single one of my own when he first came in."

The writer looked over at the guy and noticed that he had what appeared to be a slab of meat, possibly an internal organ, sitting on a napkin on the stool next to him. The man moved it up onto the bar as if to let them see it better.

He looked over and said, "Is this what you want to see? My liver? Well, here it is. I'm putting it right up on the bar, so you can get a good look."

The writer was stunned yet again. "Can everybody read minds here?" he wondered.

The liver man responded as if the writer had spoken.

"Yes, everyone can read minds. You can't have your weird thought life to yourself. You actually have to live everything in order to have any privacy. No one will notice you doing stuff, but they'll know if you're thinking about it. And I'll tell you something else. The only element of surprise here is just really blurting stuff out in the open. Then nobody sees you coming for some reason. Everyone is an idiot on the outside and a genius on the inside."

It was rare for the writer to hear English words assembled in an order that made no sense to him, so he was truly agitated by his inability to comprehend what he had just heard.

"Want another drink?" said the bartender to the liver man.

"What's the fucking difference? You know I'm never going to get drunk."

"You never know," she replied. "You should keep trying. How about something a hundred proof?"

"I don't care. Just give it to me," he whispered.

She went to the other end of the bar and took out something from under the cabinet and began to pour and pour and pour into a large glass.

The writer looked over at the liver man. "What do you mean, you can't get drunk?"

"Exactly that, buddy. I can't get drunk. I can drink as much as I want, and I will not get the relief of inebriation. Ask about the liver. This is my liver. It's my second liver. My original liver is gone, probably cremated or buried or in the trash. I got a liver transplant from somebody who was killed in a car accident, and this is the liver I got. For some fucking reason, it's not in my body, and I carry it around with me. Well, not carry around. I have it with me, as I don't move around much, just sit at the bar and try to get drunk. And I can't get drunk, so this is either some sort of alcoholic joke that the universe is playing on me, or I'm sleeping and this is a really fucked-up dream, you know, whatever. Might be my own Freudian guilty subconscious neuroses or whatever. My version of your creepy dream about dating your mom."

The writer could feel sweat beading around his temples as he mustered the strength to speak. "I wasn't dreaming about dating my mom."

"No," said the liver man with a smile, "you weren't dreaming about it. You were actually planning it."

"Am I having some sort of hallucination, some severe irony-heavy hallucination? Do you think you could be a little more helpful and tell me what the punch line is, and then I can move on to where I'm supposed to go?"

The writer felt like he was about to throw up. He just wanted to leave. The terror that had come over him was because everything was transparent and each object and person appeared to be waiting.

At first, he had thought the bartender was in charge, but she wasn't. She was waiting too. Occasionally he'd seen her pick up the phone to make sure there was a dial tone and glance at the door to see if any other customers were coming in, but then she'd just look from the writer to the liver man, listening or waiting or something.

He knew this could not be hell for him. Maybe purgatory but not hell. It was hell for the boozing liver man, all the free drinks he could get down without so much as a buzz. But, for the writer, hell would be very different from that. It would be a perpetual date with a dumb coed he'd still want to impress and who would keep forgetting his name. Or forced karaoke. Or an eternal last sit-down with a woman he was breaking up with after cheating on her, while she told him all the things that made him a bad human being. Yes, those were the flavors of his hell. But this was hell for the kind of jerk who drank up two livers.

"Who are you to judge me? All you newcomers are the same. Looking for loopholes—terminally unique!" snapped the liver man.

"I really need some privacy to think my thoughts," the writer replied, without embarrassment this time.

The bartender gave a little laugh and said to liver man, "Come on, we have our own thoughts. Let him have his."

All three of them turned suddenly when the bell attached to the doorjamb rang as the door opened. A breeze came rushing in bearing the smell of rain, and they could hear tires driving on the street outside, that perfect swishing noise of rubber, motion, and wet asphalt. Other, more distant bells, possibly church bells, chimed far away, and leaves rustled on the branches of invisible sidewalk trees.

Someone was walking in.

*

He couldn't always tell which memories were from his first family and which were from his second. He had been a late adoption, so he still had some memories of the original people he had lived with.

One of his most vivid recollections for years, which he always assumed came from his Midwestern second family, was being at the table in his pajamas when people had come over for dinner and scratching himself uncomfortably in his pajama bottoms, until his mother calmly stopped speaking to the guests, looked over to him, and asked, "Darling, do you have an itchy penis?"

He remembered shaking his head vigorously as his bowl haircut ruffled around his head. He remembered the men at the table having the sort of haircuts that were very short on the sides and those glasses with the black tops and metal wires that encased the glass, like government-issue spectacles. A few of them wore skinny ties and black coats, and there was his mother in yellow with shiny auburn hair. He remembered knowing to be vaguely horrified when she asked about his penis, and that he knew to be horrified at such a young age was one reason he believed that the memory was from his adopted family.

Years later, when he talked to his mother about the incident, she had no memory of it. She also said they seldom had people over for dinner, and if they did it would certainly be when he was away at his cousins' house for the night, and they wouldn't have let him come downstairs in his pajamas, et cetera, et cetera.

Of course not, of course not. He should have known. That part of the story should have given it away. His Midwestern family wouldn't have let the boy downstairs in his pajamas. The mortification he remembered feeling was Midwestern, for sure, but the penis question itself, once he really thought about it, was from the time of the mysterious other family that only he knew about.

His new parents had never met them, or so they said. They knew about them through perfunctory paperwork, but the people had used fake names and a fake address, so there was no way to track them down. There were only his memories, and his imaginings, and he alone could see those mental images.

Among them were palm trees—and he was sure they were real—whether they were from Florida, California, or Hawaii, he couldn't know.

And somehow he had come to Ohio, and somehow been given to his new parents, who so very much wanted the boy. But that Midwestern life had been a chilly one. There was lightness and politeness, and there were all kinds of small talk and checking in on each other and being kind, but somehow at the heart of it was something very heavy and dark, shadowy and weighted with depression and lots and lots of weird unspoken feelings.

It was not like the stereotype of the South, with those huge family secrets and lots of boozing and that sort of thing. While there was a fair share of boozing, it was sports-related. The darkness was more a profound discomfort that seeped from the bottom of their souls, a feeling that every word had a second meaning and every sentence that was uttered actually meant something entirely different. If you could get hold of that dictionary that contained the second meanings, you might be safe. But it was nowhere to be found.

Not that he hadn't loved his childhood. He'd been passionate about books and sports, and had lots of friends. His parents had been supportive and had given him every opportunity he could want. He had a large family with many cousins and holiday rituals and laughter despite the quiet pressure to not delve too far into one's feelings. As far as adoptive families went, he'd really hit the jackpot.

But there were the memories, the weird dreams, sudden recollections, and the warm gusts of past winds he felt while walking down streets or playing on the front lawn. He remembered tottering around in a strange foyer, the man in uniform leaving by the front path or the other man, the one in the dark stage area holding the white hand of the auburn-haired mother.

The flashes of his first life always kept him slightly off-balance. He remembered the dimples on his mother's cheeks—he could see them as if in an old movie. He could even see his own chubby fingers place themselves clumsily into a soft dimple's groove. He could watch his own toddler's fingertips probing to figure out how somebody put dimples in her cheeks, how they disappeared and how they kept coming right back every time she smiled. He thought he could even remember her voice, but mostly the strongest memory was the day he fell off the couch and knocked his tooth out on the coffee table. There was blood everywhere, and his mother had come rushing into the room with the man from the theater. He remembered the look of horror on her face and her scream. He recalled a bowl of milk—she brought in a bowl of milk. She picked up his tooth from the living room floor and placed it in the bowl, and the man took it and pushed it back into his gums. And then for some reason, his mother pulled the tooth back out and said something like, "No it's a baby tooth. We have to take it out. It's just a baby tooth."

He always wondered if he remembered the scene correctly. More than with any of his other fragmentary memories. The part about the milk and putting the tooth in and taking it out seemed so cinematic as did the bloodiness of the event. There had been blood on his hands and on his mother's blouse. There had been true concern on the man's face, and even though he didn't know if he was his father, he was sure that she was his mother. No memory could top that one in potency, not even memories from his second life, or that puzzling memory of him in his pajamas. There had never been anything so dramatic in his life after that. Certainly, nothing so urgent had ever happened to him in Ohio.

He'd never seen adults running down stairs. He'd never heard hysterics or people calling for bowls of anything—let alone milk. He never heard references to pulling teeth out or putting them back in.

Those were the memories of the events of the first world. Of the world that he had to leave. Where strange things happen to children. Strange things that were similar enough to the things that happened in the second world, like losing baby teeth, but it was all more violent, and it was all more backward.

There were more questions than there were answers. The color was faded, and sometimes it would boost and move quickly like in home movies and then slow down right around when his mother's face would come into the frame of his mind, and then it would slow down more on her smile—making his stomach drop.

Still, he didn't know if these were his own memories, or whether they were the memories he had from watching movies of people watching home movies. Whether they were from books he had read where things were so incredibly descriptive that they stamped their visions in his brain. He simply didn't know. And not knowing these things had ultimately colored his entire personality.

And so on that day in the car in the garage as he was leaving—as he was leaving his body, all the questions felt on the verge of being answered, and he felt that the red-haired woman would be waiting for him. The woman who had asked him about his itchy penis. The one who smiled and made him feel silly. The one who ran to him when his tooth was knocked out while she had been off somewhere with the man upstairs. He knew in a way that the reason he was rushing to die was so that he could get to her.

He knew that he had looked for her in every woman he had cheated on and then every woman he had cheated with. He knew that he looked for her and her voice everywhere he went. He knew that every female character that he ever wrote about who was unattainable was really his lost first mother. The person who would put her fingers in his bloody mouth and feel the edges of his tooth, then pull it out again. It was only a baby tooth, she had said, and her hand had been coated with the sliminess of his spit and blood.

She would be waiting, and he wanted to believe that she would have the same concerned look on her face, that it would turn into the same smile of relief after the concern passed and she saw that he was all right. He just wanted to be with her again and know that nothing had happened between the time she had dropped him off with strangers and the time when she received him back in her arms—nothing that happened between then was of any importance to him.

*

He thought about the letters he had sent her and how one might say they were notes of passion.

He thought about when he'd broken it off with her, when she'd screamed on the telephone in a way he had never heard her speak and never imagined that she could possibly speak.

Screaming: "I'm going to post those letters on the Internet, you stupid fucking asshole!"

Thoughts like that were racing through his head. Not just about the people and the women and the students. But there was the other ridiculous woman in New York he had written to—the one with her own fan website in his honor. Not just his ex-girlfriends, all of whom he had cheated on, and not his parents, whom he so wanted to make proud even though they adored him no matter what. He thought about himself and who he was supposed to be—a writer, possibly the best living one writing in English. And then his books turned into film so even more people could swallow his words, so more people could somehow eat a part of him.

That was the thing about his depression—it was more like anxiety, and the depression was what came after the exhaustion of the spinning and running and the ruminating and the chasing of the thoughts that the anxiety produced.

It was like he was being yanked around by his arm or as if he was inside a small container with a rabid animal that was faster than him so it ran around and scratched him with its tiny little nails every time it passed his face—scratching, scratching—making crazy noises and filling his head with terrifying thoughts.

He thought about what it might be like—what it might be like to really end it all. The mere thought used to make him feel so much better, but not anymore. Now it only made him desperate for the peace and quiet that it promised. He wanted to carry the thought to action now—to not try and fix it with little things he knew might make the thought go away. He knew he couldn't smoke pot again because it brought paranoia and a living hell indescribable to those who did not experience paranoia. And he knew he couldn't drink again because it made him feel worse.

He'd gone to rehab for his drinking, and they had said, "You know, you're really just dry. Not drinking and not using drugs doesn't mean you're sober. You're just dry. Without a spiritual program, you'll go fucking bananas soon."

And maybe they had been right, but he couldn't go to those rooms. Even though he knew all it would take was leaving his brain at the door and listening to them talk about god and acceptance of a higher power so that he could find some peace and just stay alive and get some sanity—sanity that none of the pills he'd been taking could give him any longer, even though they briefly had once. Even though he knew that's all it would take, he could not bring himself to go.

He just wanted everything to go back to normal. He paced the house and tried to eat a few of the cheese crackers with the peanut butter in the middle. He looked at the dogs and how happy they were. Why couldn't he just get on all fours and join them? He thought about his old dog and how it had been the most devastating time of his life holding that animal and looking into his eyes as the doctor gently put him down. Sending him to his death—a place he had desperately wanted to go with him—to walk him into death on a long leash. The dog had been up to that point the only creature that had never confused him or made him want to hide or hate himself. The dog had never hurt him even by accident, which is how most people actually hurt him, by accident, simply by being who they were. By being human or by liking things that made him worry that perhaps they were dumb or evil and could not possibly love or even stand him. If they watched reality shows or liked big cities or didn't say please, where did that leave him?

He looked at the house he lived in. He was too self-conscious to ever have a sort of *Town & Country*–type of house or a modern sort of clean chamber house like you saw in magazines. But still, he did want it and somehow felt embarrassed that he did not have it and secretly wanted such a thing.

But it was his self-consciousness that made him more comfortable with the slightly disheveled rattiness in which he dwelled.

The earth-toned throw pillows that were tossed on the couch with the edges that were scratched, chewed, and worn down by pets, the matted dog hair on the carpet, the white rings from the glasses they used without coasters on the coffee table, and the books everywhere—books, books, books that somehow made up for the utter grotesqueness of the house. Because books were sacred. Like sacred cows among the starving, the books were pampered.

The fact that they were of the artist class made everything they used, well-used.

So he paced up and down and noticed that the Persian rugs underneath his feet were neither Persian nor particularly like rugs anymore. They seemed like flat expanses of garbage that had been rolled out with a rolling pin. Like dreadlocked animal hair tossed to the ground and made into runners, the mushy flea-bitten oriental-style red carpet took him from the kitchen to the bedroom to the living room—ultimately sticking to the bottom of his feet and holding him from moving in the hallway.

This depressed him more than he could even say. It hurt him in his soul. Yes, the carpet was soul shattering; yes, the way the photo hung above the fireplace ever so slightly crooked or how the wax from a candle had dripped and then been coated with dust— it all made him want to tear out his hair with despair. Everything was agonizing to see—everything depressed him past reason, and he didn't believe that anything could actually cheer him up again.

Nothing clean or modern or chic could give him the promise of order anymore—it simply looked clinical and made the hovel of dirt safer. Everything with any undercurrent of misery could find its own weird portal into his psyche. All the grief of the new and old lived inside him and collaborated in his suffocation and wreckage. In the old days—and there were many—things could snap him out of it, whether it was a child or a bird or some kind of a song or an idea or just that the depression would run its course and end.

But there had not been such days in months. Each thing that he put his mind to, each thing that he laid his eyes on, was taken to another level of sadness and another deeper, more horrendous version of the depression he was already in.

So, finally, his brain looped back to the letters. He tried to remember how he had been able to write a complete stranger—a strange woman—letters that opened himself up so completely to her.

How he could have trusted somebody in such a way that he could have talked about life and love and then simply put his name at the end of it all. That he had put his name at the end of his very recognizable writing style, stuck the letter in an envelope, slapped a stamp on it, and sent it on its way was what spun him out now. What on earth had he been thinking?

It was the same faith that he had in whatever new medication they would come up with at the hospital or at the therapist's office.

It was the new hope with every new shrink that he met with who told him that this approach would be good enough to crack through the steep cliffs of his misery.

It was the same hope he had whenever something new came along, something that promised to give himself back to himself or show him a sliver of a better version of himself. A hope that said that there had been some mistake and none of that self-loathing and misery was necessary—that he had misunderstood, and he was perfect, beautiful, good, and, most importantly, safe.

The faith that stopped dead at the idea of a god.

Could it have been hormones? Was it really about men being willing to do whatever was available to them in order to get themselves laid? Was it that for him the tools of his seduction were his words, and his words were what made him famous? And so his words were what would get him into the pants of some new and nubile female who would express a vague interest in him or give him some mild attention? Anything to keep his attention off his own life and his own stale miseries? Maybe a new frock to put on the same old problem. Was it a combination of hormones and the hope of the new?

This was the plight of every man, ultimately. Not just the disgusting men he had heard speak at the sex addict meetings. Maybe he was just like that one guy whose entire share had been so filled with insane mendacity that the writer had memorized it word for word just from it being seared into his brain. And, of course, the horrible man whose words would be the kicking-off point of his newest book may have just been his own horrifying doppelgänger.

He wondered if she would put the love letters on the Internet. He wondered if he should call her and beg her not to. But he hadn't heard from her in two years, and he didn't know why he was thinking about it now. He checked the Internet—googled himself and never found any of the letters he had sent her, so perhaps she threw them away or had just come to her senses and realized it was a terrible thing to do.

Of course, he hoped ultimately that she would send them back to him so he would have the solace of burning them all.

Perhaps the reason he was thinking about it was because he was thinking about his own death that day. He was thinking about what might happen should he die on that day. And, more importantly, what might happen should he die at his own hands. He thought about some of his books and the many mentions of suicide and how, without even realizing it, he would just allude to death here and there. Even in e-mails, even in casual conversations, which had made him think of letters he had sent people, which made him think of how later, should he kill himself, people would read his letters and try to see the prophetic signs.

He imagined someone saying, "He did ask quite a few questions about my thoughts on suicide, and he did make allusions to Manhattan reminding him of lemmings jumping off cliffs. I guess we should have seen it coming."

And that's what bothered him the most. The "we should have seen it coming" comments: "the troubled man"; "of course, of course, yes, there's a price for genius." And everyone would feel better, would feel less jealous about feeling quite average and not in the genius class, those not so fortunate who had to off themselves because there was a price, and the price was their life.

The writer wanted them to not think these things, and the need to control what people thought of him after his death drove him into further anxiety.

He wondered what kind of man he would have been if he'd been the kind of man who owned guns. He wondered how many years earlier he would have died had he owned a rifle. He believed he would have orchestrated a situation where he'd drive someone crazy enough to shoot him, rather than shoot himself.

He sat down in an armchair next to the fireplace that didn't work and looked out the dirty windows into the backyard. It needed some sort of landscaping out there—the backyard that the dogs had made their toilet. As much as he loved them, he realized that he lived in a giant dog bed that the dogs had taken over, and that his love for the animals had over-humanized them and made them his owners. Instead of being the leader of the pack, he had become a follower. He was at the very end of the pack—a beloved caretaker with a corner to sit in.

The rest of the place was overrun with animal hair and chew toys, and there was the overwhelming aroma of a pound.

There was deep silence save for the sound of dogs breathing, so he jumped almost clear out of his seat when the phone rang. He picked up the cordless that wasn't too far away, once he was able to locate it by listening to it ring over and over. It was under a throw on the couch across from him.

It was the phone company calling with some questions about his Internet speed. The telemarketer's voice and questions—her relentless bobbing and weaving and closing off of exits that might have allowed him to end the conversation made him almost burst into tears. The telemarketer's survival skills in the game of winning him as a customer for the new and highest imaginable speed of connectivity made him sure about what he had to do next. He ordered the upgrade from the telemarketer, to see if her victory would humanize her and thus cheer him up, and when she simply sounded even more like a hyena ripping flesh from a slow herd animal, he let himself be rude and simply hung up.

He knew then he was going to kill himself. He was tired and more tired. He was tired of the yellowing walls, tired of his own cleverness and everyone waiting every time he was about to say something, looking at him expectantly and knowing that he would never let them down by being witless. He would always amuse them. They would always think he was talking fantastic words because he was a people pleaser and he could not let them down. His work of not wanting to let anyone down began the moment he awoke and did not end until he was deep down in slumber. And if he could not sleep, then he was doomed to quietly wonder how to be liked while thoroughly hating himself.

He got up and headed over to the kitchen, went to the side door that led into the garage, and turned on the lights by pulling the string that hung from the door opener's strange motor. It seemed like a motorboat motor without the boat. He looked at the rafters and thought about hanging himself, but he was a big man. Also, it was ridiculous that he did not own any rope, and the whole belt thing seemed a bit crazy, plus it all sounded painful. He looked at the car and knew that might be the way to go. How perfect—in the gas crisis to use gas to kill yourself. How funny, he thought, and ultimately painless.

He turned on the engine to see how much gas was in the car, and the indicator showed it was full. Almost full anyway, and he thought about how much that cost to fill up so he could know the prepaid price of what he hoped would be his successful death.

He went back into the kitchen and thought awhile about if he had any booze in the house, because it would be okay to have one last cocktail while he sat out there in the garage. But there was nothing to drink, and it seemed better to go out straight anyway. He said it out loud: "Maybe it's good to go out dry."

So he got himself a large glass of orange juice and a few more of the peanut butter–filled yellow crackers on a plate and went back outside, shutting the garage door tightly behind him. He got into the passenger seat and turned on the car and just let the exhaust fill the garage. He thought about maybe it being more efficient to have a hose that you could put on the exhaust pipe and then lead back into the car through the cracked window, but again that would have involved a little bit of work, and he really wasn't in the mood for a little bit of work. He just hoped for the best, and if it didn't work, then at least he'd tried.

There was a little bit of his mind that didn't want to go, and perhaps he had hoped that he would be found unconscious and that itself would be a new hope like all the new meds used to be. The post-suicide life a happy life—where the code was cracked and, even though the depression had been so bad it had almost killed him, it had conversely cured him too like a detoxifying fever. Like a phoenix from the flame, he would come out the other side—somehow having hit bottom first.

It would all be a suicide attempt—an attempt that would fail because he had not put a hose on the exhaust pipe and led it back through the cracked window. The fact that he had let the entire garage fill with exhaust instead would save him. Somehow the cracks in the structure would let out the exhaust, and he would live, a little groggy for a few days in the hospital, but everything would be okay.

Somehow this fantasy gave him hope. Somehow this sort of cheered him—somehow this made the suicide feel sort of fun.

So he drank the juice, feeling considerably more on the positive side than he had been a few moments earlier. He thought briefly that maybe he just needed to think about killing himself again—no need to actually do it because he felt sort of okay after the full planning and ruminating thing, but as soon as he thought this, the depression came back. He noticed the cobwebs in the corners of the garage, and he started to become depressed again and believed that the only way to the other side of this thing was to try to die with the possibility of failure and salvation as a bonus.

He finished his snack and then set the plate and glass on the seat next to him. He played with the knobs and buttons on the radio and listened to the hum of the car's engine. There didn't seem to be a whole lot of exhaust building in the garage, so he just closed his eyes and lay back a little. He turned to the local public radio station and listened to the guy on the air talking during the pledge drive. Talking about money, talking about how great public radio was, talking about the writing and reading series and how without listener contributions the whole thing would go to hell in a handbasket. He listened to the voice of the radioman and felt a very distinct unease. He knew the voice, and not in a good way. But the phlegm-laden voice of the radioman faded along with everything else as the exhaust filled the concrete garage whose solid build and gapless design let out none of the gas.

It was 1999, maybe the year 2000 when he first got the letter that she sent. It was a random note, more like a scream into the abyss, and it was clear that she did not expect an answer, nor did she expect the person she addressed to ever actually receive the letter.

The letter was hysterical, and it went on and on—a pained and touching cry with its complete lack of style and form. It simply seemed that she was raw and had written to someone she had heard might be smart enough to give her an explanation. She had put it in the mailbox, and there it was, in his hands.

It was a naked letter. It was about her boyfriend cheating on her, and it was asking why and how anyone could do such a thing.

She outlined the elaborate ruse and lies—the

complete hoax the boyfriend had created to deceive her. She spelled out the horror and betrayal that she felt, and at the end of the letter, she demanded to know why.

She wanted the writer to answer her question: "Why? Why would somebody do this? I want you to tell me why someone would do such a thing? Why not just break up with me? Why not just say I don't love you? Why go to all the trouble to lie?"

The letter distracted him from almost everything else that was going on in his life—it gave him a jolt and something to be excited about. He wrote back a long typed letter that took him the better half of the day to write and rewrite and also to read and reread. Somehow he loved this girl—whoever she was. He loved her anger and how she just was full of hate and shame and swore up and down like a sailor in a note to someone she didn't even know.

He loved the sheer grit and insanity of it—the demand for an answer. As if he might actually have one. She had written to him like a child looking to her father. Yes, without realizing it, he instantly loved this letter writer.

He wrote back with all his heart, and at the top of the note he wrote "rant alert" in red. And then he proceeded to tell her all the reasons why a man would cheat on his girlfriend. Why a man would cheat on his beautiful girlfriend especially, or on the girlfriend who loved him. He berated the man who had hurt her. He defended the girl with his words, and he did what he could to explain human nature in the situation rather than delve into the personal truth of one person hurting another.

He tried to explain it to her like it was science. He tried to explain it in a way that would perhaps take some of the sting out of it for the girl—somehow help her understand that it wasn't her and wasn't personal, it was just some weird life thing.

He finally mailed the letter and then proceeded to wait in fear.

He didn't know what to think; he didn't know what to do. He was worried as soon as he sent it that the girl would get the letter and decide that, while writing to this guy was crazy, his responding was worse, and she must've been out of her mind to send him a note and invite such a rant.

But very shortly after, he got another letter from her. A longer letter—one that seemed completely intimate. She had changed tone from angry to almost entirely vulnerable and heart-stoppingly sweet and grateful for the letter he had sent.

She thanked him and said she understood, and she told him more about her feelings. She apologized for putting him in such a strange position and told him about her day and how she was dealing with things and painted a picture of her life—a place where he wasn't, a place outside his gray university office where he had been correcting papers. Her place was in New York, where he could picture her walking outside on sidewalks full of other anonymous people but separate from them because she was the one he knew. He imagined her walking her dog to the dog park while her face looked beautiful and tearstained.

He didn't know at the time, but he was being seduced—not so much on purpose—but she was writing to him the sort of things that she knew she would fall for if someone had written them to her. She gave small descriptions of the way the wood chips looked over the caked dry mud in the park. The way her hair had knotted and tangled on one side so she simply had cut it, or just the fact that the dog howled its greetings to her whenever she came home, and instead of making her feel welcome it made her feel the dog's sad life instead.

It was little details like that that made him fall for her.

And so the letters went back and forth, and so his heart got more and more entangled, and so eventually they moved on to phone calls. Long, shy, uncomfortable phone calls, which he made from his office phone, because he could not make these calls from his home since he lived with his girlfriend.

Almost from the get-go, it was obvious that what he was doing was cheating. It was the very first time he had done something like that, and the exhilaration was new and amazing, and hope was immense that this would be the person who would counter all the bad. This experience would be what would ultimately lift him out of the low-level rain that drizzled in his life.

The hope for this sort of salvation had in the past taken the form of scholarships and writing awards and the clocking of all kinds of achievements, and, of course, the hope had taken the form of relationships with new girlfriends—but only slightly and never beyond the average sort of expectation. But the hope had never been this bold or taken the shape of an unknown person from far away who by some twist of fate had been cast before him. The hope had never taken the shape of serendipity.

And so the hope had renewed itself through this exotic stranger and with great intensity. She felt like a drug, and he wanted to chop her up and snort her to feel her more. To feel her faster.

He thought about her day and night, and as the time approached for his trip to Washington, DC, to help pick the award winners for the National Endowment for the Arts, he could only think of how close he would be to New York and to where the girl was.

He casually wrote her about his trip to DC in a note without outstepping their current bounds, which firmly pretended they were forming a casual friendship. A friendship that was somehow propelling them to write multipage letters that they sent through the US Postal Service. And he added that if she was in the DC area during the time of his trip, he would hope that she'd let him take her out for a meal.

She had written back, of course, saying that she would love that. He immediately launched eagerly into the exact time and location of his DC visit. And once she said that she would make sure she was in the area, that she would take a train to put herself in the area, the ball rolled into the territory of sex.

There was now no more hiding that they were embarking on an affair, and there was no more hiding that they were about to have a rendezvous and that this was indeed a romantic union. Their flimsy fake friendship was not a friendship. Quickly they became giddy with the idea of staying at their meeting place and getting two hotel rooms just to be tasteful. The excitement of getting to know each other became amplified into something almost approximating anxiety and fear—high-pitched emotions that kept them both awake at night. And when he was kept awake, he was kept in a state of agitation so acute that he actually had to try and mask it with dramatized colds and headaches and other physical ailments so as not to be caught in the raw feelings by his girlfriend.

He was almost hysterical. He was way too nice to his girlfriend, touching her way too much. He was over-loving his partner out of the sheer inability to direct his excitement about the New York girl anywhere else. He directed it to the person he should have been giving the attention to in the first place. And for a brief while, she got to enjoy what was indeed the love that he was feeling for another woman until the time came for his trip.

He made multiple phone calls and arrangements and received train information from the New York girl. He would be arriving on the day before her train came, and he would reserve a room for her in the same hotel where he was being put up by the organization who hired him to help choose the recipients of the writing prizes—not gallivant around with a girl.

They had gone over how he would meet her at the gate at the train station, and she had tried to tell him what she would be wearing and what she looked like, and this, in turn, made things even more carnal and uncomfortable. She described her dress, then stopped and laughed, and he said to her, "Please don't wear a lethal dress," which was the most charming thing any man had ever said to her.

And that's how it really started, his confession that her dress would perhaps be his undoing. There was no turning back.

He arrived at the station and saw someone he assumed was her walking off the train and down the hall of the terminal, then ducking into a ladies room and coming back out a few moments later with a darker shade of lipstick on. And it was confirmed that it was her when she saw him too, recognizing him from his book jacket, then smiling and quickening her pace towards him.

He felt immediately disappointed—not because she wasn't beautiful, because she was. But she was not heart-manglingly beautiful in that way that he had only imagined—in that way that he had never seen before and had thought that, if he met a woman of such beauty, somehow he would never feel depressed again. He knew it was absurd, but he had secretly thought that such a woman would make it so he would never be afraid again: her mere physicality would ensure that nothing could ever go wrong with the same intensity for the man she chose.

No, the New York girl was human. She was very attractive, but she was not some creature from another time and place who would transport him away from himself and into a new stratosphere of godliness.

He could not remember how they greeted one another since his head was so much louder than the occasion.

She stood and looked up at him as he looked down at her, and he could see their mouths moving and greetings being exchanged, but he heard nothing.

Eventually, the echo and the underwater sounds gave way to real voices, and he heard himself say something funny. He saw her laugh a tiny bit and heard the sound of her voice in person, and that was that.

And before he knew it—before he could be fully present and engage her in a real conversation—he found himself wondering if she too was disappointed.

He started to believe that he could read her

mind, that she was thinking the same things that he was. That this young and beautiful girl was thinking this man could not possibly make up for the pain she had hoped he would make up for. That nothing he could do could erase what had recently happened to her at the hands of another man.

He started imagining that he could see her already beginning to be nice for kindness' sake, so as not to be rude or to hurt his feelings.

He felt like he was about to have a full-blown panic attack but calmed down long enough to hear her ask him a question. She said:

"What's in the backpack?"

He was carrying a large, heavy, overstuffed backpack—very strange and inappropriate for a quick trip to the train station.

He simply smiled and said to her in his best aw-shucks way, "a first aid kit." She slowly began to smile and then started to laugh in a very genuine and heartfelt way, grabbing his arm slightly as she leaned forward and dropping her head while her laughter picked up and became more guttural.

That's when he knew that it was going to be okay—at least for a while. That if she was able to laugh as hard at that, at a pointless bit of humor, then they were going to be comfortable partners for the brief time they would know each other. He already knew that their time together would be brief, and although he wanted it to be brief, he also hoped, as they walked out of the station, that she would not feel the same and would be sorry about the way things would eventually turn out.

Chapter Two

Mrs. Randall

SHE SAT UP IN THE LARGE BED, waking from the long dream she'd been having. Dwight had been in the dream with her, but she woke up alone, and her heart sank as it did each morning, knowing she had to be in that bed between those cool sheets looking out the window of the new house and not being able to share her thoughts with him. She ran her hands over her belly and then swung her legs over the end of the bed, plopping down to the floor. The bed was a little bit high for her, but she managed to slip into her fluffy slippers, pull on her nightgown, and wobble over to the bedroom door. She looked back at the window and the balcony, but it still hurt too much to go out and look at the birds and the view without Dwight.

The baby was kicking that morning. The two of them would have breakfast without Dwight, and she was already prepared for that melancholy and did not want to make it worse with the view from the bedroom.

She opened the heavy door with its brass doorknob and slowly walked down the stairs to the kitchen, where she would make eggs and coffee, and perhaps a little bacon for herself since she'd been craving it for a few days after smelling the next-door neighbor's cooking.

She also heard all the kids clamoring in and out of the neighbors' back door and into their yard. Somehow she associated a full house with the smell of bacon and felt silly making just enough for one, but still the dog looked hungry. He had come in through his door and was standing there waiting for a treat or some sort of answer, eyes large and expectant. She looked at him and said, "Do you miss Dwight too?"

She put the coffee on to boil, went over to the kitchen table, and sat down. The kitchen tiles were a little bit sparse for her—a little too white next to the cabinets, which were a dark wood she liked a lot. She liked the built-in cabinetry—it really was a clever way of designing a house, with a premade plan that you bought so you didn't have to think it all up yourself.

She put her feet up on a chair and rubbed her belly, gently touching the baby while she smoked her morning cigarette. She figured out where his butt was, where his arms were, and his shoulder and head too. As she breathed in the tobacco smoke, she could feel him calming; it was a calming cigarette, one that she looked forward to in the morning—and then again after lunch and in the evening sitting out on the porch after having made dinner for one. If none of the girls came to visit her, she would have a little drink anyway with or without them. Maybe some brandy, or she'd mix herself a martini with that lovely silver shaker. It was all right, she'd think, Dwight would be home soon. How long can they deploy someone, anyway?

It was the trips to the grocery that were the hardest. She believed that sometimes women looked at her with a certain pity that they wouldn't feel if she wasn't pregnant. As if perhaps her husband had some choice in leaving and had opted to abandon her. She believed that some women thought that perhaps he could've stayed on and helped her while she was pregnant. She believed she could read the judgment in their eyes but also knew her self-pity could play tricks on her.

Others knew that that's just how it was—the military wives, the ones who already had kids—they knew that nobody waited for a pregnant woman. Men had their jobs. The woman ran the family, and the man would come and go. He had to go.

She ran her fingers through her red hair as she finished the cigarette. Her hair was cut short, and she wondered if perhaps she should let it grow out a little. She checked her face in the oven door and thought she looked a little pale.

"Perhaps you should have some orange juice or some tomato juice," she thought out loud. "Maybe you can go visit the neighbors. Maybe give your mother a call and maybe let your family come and take care of you a little more."

She was, after all, seven months pregnant. Seven

months and few weeks, actually, so the baby would be coming soon. It was getting harder and harder to do household chores, and the garden had certainly gone to seed. The little man who came to pull the weeds and tend to the flowers and trees was a bit older than she'd realized. A while ago, she'd noticed that he'd hurt himself and had to sit quite a bit. So she'd given him the day off, and then he took the week off, and before she knew it a few weeks had passed and there was no sight of him. The vines were beginning to crawl, and the weeds were beginning to take over and touch the sides of the house. She felt that she was slowly being cocooned within the walls of the house by the wild and hungry garden.

She looked at the lace curtains, and they looked dingy. She knew she would have to get on a chair to take them down to bleach and wash. There was nothing worse than dingy white curtains to make a house look wilted. But she thought that perhaps it was not such a good idea to climb on a chair. So instead she wandered around the house looking at all the things that needed repair and cleaning and smoked another cigarette slowly, holding her coffee in the other hand. Finally, she sat down on the stairs and began to cry.

She put the cigarette out in her coffee, put both on the ground, took her head and face in her hands, and sobbed loudly. This was not what she had had in mind for herself. This was not fair, she thought, that her dreams, her plans had been taken from her. Why on earth should she be home alone? Why on earth did she have to live through this, and how was she not to worry as the doctor kept telling her? Not worry about what to do with the baby when he was born. Was she going to do it without Dwight? When, when, when would he be coming home?

She put on the yellow dress that she wore almost every day without any care. It was increasingly difficult to button the back buttons, so she just left them open and let her brassiere show. She vigorously brushed her hair and put on a straw hat, then slipped her feet into her white flats and headed out to the front yard.

She walked down the path to the gate and opened it, and she stood on the sidewalk for a moment looking left to right. She looked at the car and decided against driving, since her belly was in the way and she had to push the seat back too far for her hands to reach the steering wheel. So she started to walk and thought, "Where on earth am I going?" She trudged on, even though the nearest store was a mile away on Glendale, but she decided to see if somebody would give her a ride back once she got there.

When she reached the store, she was damp with sweat. The people in the shop looked worried and had her sit down on a little stool, and they asked her what it was that she needed. She gave them her shopping list, and they began filling up a bag with all the provisions—canned goods, bread, and a few things for herself like hairspray and rouge. The heat hadn't helped during the walk, and they could tell that perhaps she'd been crying because of the redness around her eyes. Because of her red hair and skin coloring, she couldn't hide her emotional meltdowns—her eyes would stay pink, her lips would swell up, her cheeks would turn bright orange, and her freckles would show themselves more prominently than usual—all pointing to the fact that she'd either been crying or was experiencing something major inside her head.

The storekeepers' son gave her a ride back to her house in his black truck. The customers wished her well, and the store gave her some extra jam to take home. Before she knew it, she was at the front path again, the truck was driving away, and the son was waving goodbye to her. She had hoped for a longer journey before standing on the path leading to her house. She stood alone wondering, what next?

She went inside and sat down on the couch, dropping the groceries on the floor for the dog to come and sniff at. She looked around at the large fireplace, the curtains that needed bleaching, the bare walls. She had been thinking of getting wallpaper but suddenly knew what she really wanted. Paintings. Paintings of people. Paintings of people who looked like they were in love—maybe lovers dancing. Baby paintings. Paintings of picnics and strange birds. Paintings of regal women who didn't look afraid and men who've come back from wars. She whispered, "I want paintings."

She'd been reading *Life* magazine, and there'd been an article about bohemians in New York, bohemians in Paris, and all the painters in all their studios and art galleries having shows. She knew that they sold their work, and all she had to do was contact a gallery. She certainly had the money to buy some art, so why not do it?

Why not start doing that sort of thing? Going to salons, going to places where there were lots of people milling about and no one putting you in a truck and making sure you got home like a lost dog. Where they let you stay and talk, talk about things that weren't even in front of you but just in your head. She decided to reread the article and picture herself as a part of it. When she had first read it, she had felt so small and embarrassed—like a dummy. But she remembered that she had done well in school, gotten good grades. So why couldn't she like paintings and use her money to have them?

The article had said that all those artists were scrappy and poor. That they lived in lofts and garrets. That they shared everything they had with each other. It was astounding to her that somewhere that sort of freedom existed—the freedom to love everybody and to not have to pretend that some people were inappropriate for you and some people were just there to shake hands with and move on from instead of to really get to know. She wanted to explore the experience of knowing anyone she wanted. Maybe art was the key. Now, where could she find these things, and how on earth could she get her hands on some art, go to openings where people wore foreign clothes and hugged strangers and other people's wives?

Well, she simply had to find out.

She sat up, got off the couch, and walked around the room looking for where she had tossed the magazine. It was by the ottoman, and she bent over with difficulty to pick it up off the floor. She lifted it up, opened to the page where the article was, and started to skim through it before poring over it. By the end of the first page, she realized that the article gave the names of the galleries, the streets and the restaurants and taverns these artists frequented, and most of these places were in New York.

She decided that the moment was important. She felt a strange weight lift from her very being. The truth was that, when she thought about the art and the galleries and painters, she no longer missed Dwight and had no interest in bleaching the curtains. So she thought she would write to them. She would write to the galleries. She would tell them that she wanted art and she wanted paintings.

That is how it all began.

Mrs. Dwight T. Randall began her fanciful art collection on a hot summer day after being dropped off at home by a grocery boy.

She was wide-eyed with wonder, seven months and a few weeks pregnant, and the loneliest she'd ever been. But when she had the idea of wanting to put art on her walls, and when she connected it with the articles she had read and all the spirit with which the artists did what they did, her loneliness lifted, and she would never feel it in that same way again.

*

It seemed impossible to believe that Dwight was coming back in one day. After all, he'd been gone for so many days and there had been so many different stages to his absence and to her adjustment to his absence that for him to return all at once, in one day, in one hour, in one minute, and to cross the threshold of their home all in one step, seemed like too much.

It seemed like he should come back in bits and pieces. Maybe first his voice should come back, then his luggage, and then his body for an hour or two and only in one room or possibly only on the front step—not even in a room—and then he would slowly move in. But for him to come back with all his things and all his personality and voice and smells all at once—she felt like she would be steamrolled.

Flattened out with emotion and sensation, all the things that a person and everything they mean to you can do to you when they are nearby.

She wondered what he would think of the art she had bought and put on the walls, from top to bottom.

She wondered what he would think of the peasant skirt she'd been wearing instead of the store-bought skirts the ladies wore around town, and the new friends she had and how they came over and ate barbecue and read their poetry aloud.

She had a feeling it would all be changing. She had a feeling Dwight might like the espresso maker—the little aluminum metal pot you pressed the coffee grinds into. She had certainly spent a bit of money getting some of the best Italian coffee and boiling the water and pouring it through to make that real strong shot. The kind she'd gotten used to drinking in the mornings with her friends who often spent the night sleeping on the couch and in the spare rooms. It was a very big house. God, she knew he would think it was indecent, and she would have to lie.

The truth was that there was an ever-growing part of her that did not want Dwight to come back. But he was coming back, and the baby had been born and wasn't even a baby anymore. He was a little boy, wandering around the house in his diaper, talking his baby talk with a lot of different people who'd become familiar to his baby eyes. People who weren't his uncles and aunts and certainly weren't his grandparents. People who clicked their fingers and wore rosewater perfumes and thought war was bad but art was great.

And she thought they were great with their cigarettes, hand-rolled and slim. She didn't want to give up this bohemian life she'd created in the house. She did not want to live with the soldier her husband had become. She wondered if he could join her in the art life, the life of paintings and parties.

Perhaps he would like Giovanni and Pamela with her crazy hair, and perhaps he would like the friends she had made in San Jose when she'd gone to see the artists. They were showing work out of her house now. They invited all kinds of people over to meet her, and they ate homemade bread and stayed up late telling stories and smoking in a circle around the fire.

On the day Dwight was returning, the house was shining from bottom to top. The wood was polished to a reflective sheen, and the curtains that had been dingy had finally been bleached. New sheets were put on the marriage bed, the furniture had been swept of ash and dusted, and the tables were covered with vases of roses and bowls of fruit. The carpets had been beaten outside and the floors waxed and oiled. That was apparently what you were supposed to do when someone returns—clean the house within an inch of its life.

She paid one of her artist friends to rake the yard, and she'd had a few of the girls come over and help her bake so the house could smell good for him. She made dinner and put out some wine and a little bit of whiskey and some cigars she'd managed to get hold of as she sat and waited for Dwight.

Their boy looked beautiful. He was a sweet-tempered child and was wearing his little pants and sailor shirt. It was all very exciting and horrible. Her heart was in her throat. Then she heard the door opening.

She didn't know why she was waiting for the doorbell to ring. After all, Dwight would not have rung the doorbell since it was his house. But still, she was startled and somewhat offended and briefly upset when she simply heard the front door open.

He should have rung the doorbell. He had not been living there for close to three years and was coming back into her life. Was he just going to walk in like he owned the place?

She stopped cold in her tracks in the kitchen before heading down the hall to meet him. He did own the place, and he owned the child that she had, and everything around her was his. He even owned her— she was not her own person, although sleeping with other men while Dwight was gone had made her feel that way briefly.

After all, she didn't pay for any of it. It was his money she bought the artwork with.

He did own the house, and he had a key to it, and he was coming back to take possession of it and her.

She thought all this in a split second and immediately sank into a deep resentment. She was having all the wrong feelings, something she had not known infidelity would bring about. Shouldn't she be soaring with love for her husband because he was her husband? Did her body not know this? Did it simply have marriages of the flesh? Shouldn't she be running to the front door to meet her man, their baby under her arm?

She was simply frozen in the hall.

The child and the dog ran to the front door. She heard Dwight's voice, deep and familiar, and she heard the little squeaky voice of her son. There was a quiet, a hush, and she knew Dwight would be gently patting the boy's head and looking at him. She knew that he would not grab the boy. He would first say as she heard him say,

"Hi, Jimmy. I'm your dad. Do you feel like giving me a hug?"

Tears rolled down her cheeks when she walked out and saw them. Dwight immediately walked over to her and put his arms around her waist, pulling her close to him. In a way, it was rough and strange. His starched uniform felt coarse. He smelled like meat or an animal, and then there was the cosmetic smell of whatever it was that was in his hair and the distant smell of whatever it was he had had in his mouth and eaten hours before.

She could taste and smell and feel, and it was all too much. So when she did faint, when everything turned to darkness, and she felt like she was doing a somersault into a swimming pool but was instead sliding down towards the polished floor, anyone would've thought it was from the joy and excitement of seeing her husband. But in fact, it was from sensory overload and a vague repulsion from his physical being. It was from not being able to handle what was happening to her. It was only the toddler's yowls that made her want to wake up from her faint and participate.

After they put Jimmy to bed, they sat in the kitchen and talked.

He talked for what seemed like hours, and she made him some of her strong coffee, which he seemed to like. He smoked a strong filterless cigarette and was surprised to see that she had her own to smoke but said nothing.

He watched her move around a little, cutting some of the pie she'd heated and putting it on a plate. He cut his second helping himself. She saw the way he cut the pie and how it was different from the way she cut it. She saw how he put the knife on the counter instead of in the sink so the crumbs from the knife landed on the counter and she would have to wipe it up later since she didn't want to wipe it right then and be rude. But she kept thinking about the crumbs and the sweetness of the crust sitting there on the counter and maybe ants coming, and she wondered why he didn't just put it in the sink. It would've been so easy. The sink was right next to where he put the knife down, and she felt irritated and helpless. She thought this is it—this is the new deal—him putting things where they don't belong and her having to follow him around to put them back.

She felt like her breathing was getting heavy and deep from thinking about these things. She thought about how he didn't use a saucer and kept putting the cup down on the table. She tried to remember that he'd been in the military and had just gotten home, and she was being small spirited. She was supposed to just love him, but it was hard.

If one of her artsy friends put a cup down without a saucer she'd simply copy him because it meant it was nifty—so why was she so critical of the man who paid for all the cups and coffee and tables to begin with?

He commented on her hair and how he liked it. He called it "different." He mentioned that her skirt was nice and flowing and that it reminded him of what some of the women in the villages he'd been deployed to wore.

This made her think about the stories of romances between soldiers and the young local women in the towns where they were stationed. The whole thing made her stomach hurt. It was the only proof she had that perhaps she still loved him. Jealousy was the only thing that connected her to what might be a physical attraction to the man.

He did have new lines on his face, lines around his mouth. Some were laugh lines, or maybe they were cringe lines and frown lines. She reached out and touched them with her fingers, and the tenderness of the gesture made him excited but embarrassed too. It felt like they were newlyweds. He did not know how to approach the subject of physicality, and neither did she, so they held hands at the kitchen table and talked until dawn. Then around four or five, they fell into their bed.

He commented on the cleanliness of the sheets and how he could not believe he was there. She went to put on some cream and prepare herself for his advances, but when she came back, she found him fast asleep. She climbed into bed, pulled the covers up to her neck, and listened to him breathe. He turned on his side and pulled all the covers with him. This was new, too.

She pulled on the covers and tried to get them back by putting her weight on the edge and yanking, but she could not. She lay there with half of one cover in the open air and fretted. She wondered how long it would take to get used to this.

She drifted to sleep but only for a few hours. Jimmy woke up crying, and she got up to feed him and change his diaper. Even though he was a toddler, he was still not potty trained, and she knew that Dwight would probably take care of all that in one week. Dwight wouldn't stand for it; he'd be a soldier in the house.

There was something about him, something

changed about him, but it didn't matter since she couldn't remember what he was like before. She simply felt like she was in this new thing with Dwight again, just as she had come to enjoy her own life for the very first time.

She went downstairs and started to cook breakfast. She put the baby in his chair, smoked, and watched him while she waited for Dwight to wake up.

He slept for hours. He slept until two in the afternoon. He slept so long that she thought, maybe this could work. Maybe this new life of hers would be okay and Dwight would be there, and he'd simply be sleeping, or at work. Maybe she would be able to see her new friends, be able to keep collecting art, and have little barbecues where they cooked food from interesting countries, tried new things, read essays, and listened to music on the old record player, and even danced a little. Maybe Dwight would be shy and resigned and would step away and let her do such things and let her stay like a daughter downstairs while he slumbered forever upstairs.

Maybe it would be like that.

*

Dwight's absence had been the longest three years of her life. At first, there was the daunting idea of him being gone and possibly getting killed, but then the time had become her own. Three years. And once the time became hers, that is when each minute of every day had become filled with an entire universe's worth of revelations.

She hadn't been Mrs. Randall for very long when Dwight had to leave, so she hadn't been used to the matronly way that she was looked at after becoming married and then quickly pregnant. She would create outside errands to keep busy, frequently going to get her shoes resoled or to have her hats re-stitched.

She would always note the Alex Theatre right next door to the shoe store. A place she had gone to as a child to see shows with her family but hadn't really given much thought to since. Occasionally there would be a movie there, and she'd try to get Dwight to go, but he was always busy with his work, engrossed in his cold steam or whatever kind of energy he was working on for the government. But one time, after Dwight went away and she had life to herself, she went by to drop off some shoes to be fixed and glanced up at the Alex to see what films were playing. Maybe she could catch a matinee—drop the baby off with the neighbor and go off by herself.

That would have been exciting, she thought. Maybe she could call up one of her girlfriends who wasn't busy with her own family—not that anyone was able to come out and play with her these days, since her friends had always been older and their husbands were older and not enlisted men. Her own brothers and sisters had all dispersed, and since she'd been the baby, she was left behind. Her parents had passed, and

Dwight was really the only family she had, and all his family was in Oklahoma. So, not a lot of matinee companions for her to call on.

She thought, "Well, this won't kill you. It's like starting off in a new grade. You can make new friends. Even just one would be fine. Maybe a girl who works in a shop, and you can go to see the pictures with her. In the meantime, you can go alone."

She thought all this while standing outside the theater. Then she realized that the Alex Theatre wasn't showing a film. It was advertising a local production of a play that would be playing there soon, but it didn't say when. She moved towards the little ticket office, which was closed, to see if there was a date posted there, but all she saw was a poster that said: "Volunteers Needed for Production."

She took out a pencil and wrote down the phone number—she didn't even know why, but she did. Then she headed back home. She jumped on the bus, took it as close to home as she could, and then walked the rest of the way, back to the neighbor's house, where she picked up Jimmy.

Once she was back inside her kitchen, she looked at the number she'd written down. She held it in one hot, gloved hand and wondered why she'd written it down and what it was that people volunteered to do there.

She wondered if perhaps she could help sell tickets at the theater, or maybe she could serve the refreshments. Something like that would certainly pass the time, and it would be an exciting and cheap way to meet other women in her position who might want to be friends.

And if it was in the evenings, or maybe during the days or whenever, the neighbors could certainly mind the baby. They seemed very enchanted with the toddler. They were trying to have one last baby since their big kids were busy and running around and not quite as cuddly as they used to be.

And so she dialed the number, and after waiting and listening to it ring over and over again, she got someone on the line. The person responded to her query about volunteering very quickly, as if she couldn't stay on the phone. She told her to come down tomorrow at three and stay there for a few hours and help out. She didn't say with what. So she told the theater woman that she would be there, since it would have been impolite to say no or ask further questions and seem picky or arrogant.

The next day she dropped Jimmy off with their neighbors, walked down to Main Street, hopped on the next bus, and got all the way down to the Alex. She got out, excited, in her best dress, gloves, and hat, crossed the street, and went up to the theater door. She banged on the glass till someone inside saw her, came over, and opened the door for her.

She was led to the back of the theater by the ticket boy and then shown through a side door in the back of the house. She suddenly entered a room through what could have been a black hole in space because the theater was so dark. To her amazement, the room was full of about a dozen people of both sexes sitting around. Some had coffee, and one was playing with a feather duster, but all of them were busy doing various things.

There was a woman sewing, there was somebody cutting fabric, someone drawing plans on paper, and there was somebody stretching her body in the oddest way. Almost like stretching her legs but at the same time stretching her back, with her torso facing down to the ground. She was a little startled when the person stood up straight. It wasn't a woman at all; it was a man.

"So, you must be Mrs. Randall," said the heavyset woman who had been cutting fabric and who sounded like the person she had spoken to on the phone. "And you've come here to volunteer with us? You certainly are dressed up, for a volunteer. Where to begin? We have some overalls you can wear somewhere—right, Joe?"

The man who had been stretching gave an affirmative grunt in response. She looked over at him, looked more intently at his face. He was beautiful in a way she was unaccustomed to in men. He had creamy, coffee-colored skin and warm, warm eyes.

He stepped out into the light—his hair was slicked back a little bit, and his hands were long, slender, and well-manicured.

He smiled slowly. She caught a glimpse of his teeth and knew her face was burning red and that there was nothing much she could do about it.

The darkness of the backstage area masked her face, but for the life of her, she could not understand her reaction. She certainly hoped it was not going to be a reoccurring thing.

"I'll be needing some help with the sets, but I think we're covered in every other area," he said. "So unless you object to a little paint, we can get started right away. Here are your overalls."

When he spoke these words directly to her, she blushed again. This time his diction, so precise, had taken her off guard. She felt immediately ashamed about being surprised by this—as if she had assumed his diction shouldn't be wonderful.

"Why wouldn't it be?" she admonished herself in her head. "He's an American and has gone to American schools. He went to the same school as I did maybe, and probably got great grades. Why shouldn't he speak well?"

"Mrs. Randall?" his voice came again.

"Yes, that would be fine, yes, yes," she said.

"We'll see you in a bit," he called back to the sewing woman as he led the way to the tarp and paints on the stage.

And that's how it started. She put on some ridiculous men's overalls and someone's tennis shoes and was handed a paint roller and some brushes. She just copied the stretching man, whose name was Joe. She helped Joe paint the sets and cut wood into the shapes of trees, with green at the tops where they were cut in rounded powder-puff shapes as if the tops of trees were not all that different from the tops of imaginary clouds. It wasn't very accurate, but everyone knew what those shapes meant.

Every day she went in, and she painted small details in large details and great swabs of blue sky and earth, and she felt when she left that she was a slightly different person.

She would come home and find herself a slight bit impatient with Jimmy. Suddenly he was being a baby, needing her to hold him and help him all the time, which didn't seem so appealing. He didn't seem like a little doll anymore but more like a whining animal that could not take care of itself.

She wanted baby Jimmy to be old enough to draw great pictures and to be creative and to talk to her, but he wasn't. He was helpless and needed shaping like clay, but she was busy being shaped herself. She felt that there was nothing she wanted to impart to Jimmy about her old self, and there was an impasse where she dared not teach him anything, because she felt like she herself had not learned it and it might be wrong.

But she was learning. She would go back to the theater every other day and paint, slowly starting to talk a little with Joe and with the seamstress and listen to them talk about their jobs. Then the actors eventually streamed in and started to rehearse and do some of that stretching she'd seen Joe do. It turned out Joe was a performer, and he'd do a bit of rehearsing, stretching his singing voice with the play's songs.

The stage was almost done, and before she knew it two weeks, then three weeks had passed. She felt closer to these people than she had to anyone in some time and laughed at the idea that she had thought she would make friends with shop girls and go to see films. She felt beyond that girl-outing nonsense.

She felt a quick and strong bond with these people. They talked about things that were highly personal—things that would not have been okay to talk about with her friends who had husbands and children. They talked about their feelings and disappointments. They talked about people in their families who drank too much, and they talked about loneliness and anger.

They talked about everything you could think of, and they joked around a lot and would kid each other in the cleverest ways. They would say things that other people might think rude, but the person they'd say it to would laugh and see it as a sign of love. They even teased her about being an unhappy housewife and about sneaking out when her man was away, leaving the baby hungry and dirty at home. At first, she had been horrified and tried to defend herself, but then she realized that it was a joke, and in a way, it made her feel loved.

When they were joking with her, the lady she'd first talked to would chuckle deeply and give her a reassuring look while cutting fabric or peddling her foot up and down on her Singer sewing machine. They would all reassure her kindly, each and every one. Even the guy who did the lights and the one who pulled stuff back and forth—things she didn't even know the names for.

The most amazing thing about that place was how often they told her she was beautiful. Not in that way that her husband or the neighbors did. Not that "Honey, you look nice, doesn't she look nice?" kind of thing. The theater people told her she looked beautiful with specific examples of why, and they made it sound rare and exotic. It made her feel like a movie star. They made her see herself like she hadn't before.

One of them talked of the cupid's bow of her lips being so sharply drawn that only God could have been so precise. Or that the waves in her hair were like mattress springs; somehow, they made that sound great. Everybody would start laughing if the compliment was clumsy, but they'd smile too because they knew what was meant, and they knew that Mrs. Randall was happy to hear it.

Over the next three years, she volunteered and helped and eventually made a little money with the theater. And so it was that she fell in love with Joe and he with her. It was only natural that they became a couple. Within the theater, it was absolutely fine, as it was in his apartment on Louise Street where they made love and cooked dinner together in his tiny kitchen. He hardly ever came to her house or saw little Jimmy, and she tried to not think about how to handle her husband returning home from abroad.

She knew that going to the theater would have to be negotiated with Dwight when he came back, and she felt that she would not give up Joe under any condition. She did not feel torn. When she thought about it, she saw that Dwight had left her for too long. He had written letters containing details of airplanes, details of meals, but he had never once written to say he loved her and that her hair was like joyful bedsprings or that the cupid's bow of her lips was all he could think about, because that was not who he was and it was *not* all that he could think about.

Dwight was busy thinking about cold steam engines, airplanes, and war. And even when he had been at home, she realized he had been obsessed with the Grand Central air terminal in Glendale, obsessed with the various functions of the terminal and all the accompanying logistics.

He had also been obsessed with getting things right in the house and with just the sort of shellac the stairs needed to make them shiny and reflective. As far as she was concerned, he made the steps treacherous, and the meticulous chores that he concerned himself with were never of any use to her.

So she was in many ways quite lonely and had been so before Dwight had even left. And whether this was the rationalization of an adulteress or not, she had decided that she did not care. She had found love. She had found a man with whom she could sit on a porch and talk about life with and laugh. He touched her gently and listened to her and asked questions. In all seriousness, he would smile and tell her that she did a good job at the theater, that she was doing something she'd gotten good at, perhaps something she should keep on doing.

She knew that this was the life she needed and to go back to a life without that kind of companionship and encouragement would surely kill her. She felt that it was her God-given right to have art in her world and it was her God-given right to gently hold Joe's hand and it was her God-given right to be young and to be loved.

*

It had taken Dwight a while to settle in. In a way, she knew that all she had to do was to get him back into a routine so that she could then go back to her own routine, the one she'd created without him.

Dwight at first was not happy with how she had spent some of the money he had left her. He was not happy with the art in the living room, and he was not happy with her working at the theater while leaving little Jimmy with the neighbors. But in time he grew to accept these things, because he loved her and liked it when she was happy, and in time he had his own preoccupations and began to not notice her comings and goings. As long as Jimmy was not underfoot, he didn't mind. Soon she was taking Jimmy to the theater with her anyway. Dwight believed that, historically, women had always been drawn to and enjoyed art and theater, so why should he object?

Dwight went back to being an engineer for the government, finding solutions to issues with cold steam. He would go to Pasadena to work out problems with other engineers. He was happy when dinner was on the table when he got home. His wife still kissed him affectionately, and he saw that she was interested in what she did, and she certainly didn't force him to go to the playhouse to see any of the things she was working on.

She'd tell him about the friends she'd made in the theater, though, and that amused him. Occasionally she would mention a man, but Dwight noticed that she would mention him in passing as though she did not really know him very well. This made sense to Dwight, since the males at the theater probably worked in men's areas, like carpentry and the outside types of things that a theater might need.

That made him feel a little better about things, since at first it had made his stomach clench to think of her around strange men. Dwight was old-fashioned, but he knew the world was changing and moving ahead, so he hoped he'd learn to be open to that change. He did not want to be like his own father back in Oklahoma, who had been unwilling to see the tide changing in life and so had stayed stuck.

*

Dwight had been looking for something for what seemed like days. She wasn't sure if it was a sketch or a document or one of the parts to one of his projects. She had been way too distracted to think about what it was or to help him. It had seemed like a much better idea to simply stay out of his way.

She came home at around three in the afternoon on a Wednesday after having been at the theater. She'd started to help one of the women, one of the newer ones, with wardrobe fittings, and it had been fun. Joe had written another poem for her, and the passion in it had been powerful, so she had a little joy in her step as she walked in the front door.

Having now become a seasoned adulteress, she knew how to take that happiness home to her husband and make it be about him. She walked into the foyer and shut the front door behind her, its glass rattling ever so slightly. The A-line of her coat billowed out a little from the door closing quickly, and she began to unpin her hat to put it on the hall table. She looked at her own reflection and smiled and called out, "Where are you, honey?"

Dwight had taken the day off from work. He had been working in his home office and catching up on some household bills and paperwork. So he was probably somewhere in the house digging around for that thing that he was looking for again.

She had a passing feeling in her stomach—a flutter, a quick flutter—and she put her hat down on the side table and called out again.

"Honey?"

She scurried into the kitchen but couldn't find him and came around to the living room and back down to the hallway. She looked up the stairs and suddenly, with a start, saw that he was standing at the top, looking down at a piece of paper in his hands.

"Honey?" she called up again. But she recognized quickly that something was very wrong, and right after, she recognized the color and texture of the paper he was holding.

He was holding a letter and had been reading it. His fingers were crushing the edges—even from the bottom of the stairs, she could see that he had been reading and rereading it for quite some time.

"Dwight?" she said with urgency and something of a stern tone to make him snap out of it and look at her, and he did. He looked at her, and he said evenly:

"I found these letters in your closet. I found these letters from a man, and I think they're love letters and I think that I really don't understand or believe or…. I just don't know what to say. I don't know what to do. I just don't want this to be happening. I just want this to not be true."

She took a step to move up towards him, but he flinched and said, "No, please don't." And in that moment his foot, which was clad only in a sock and had been hanging off the top step, slipped a little as she watched.

She thought of Jimmy and how often they told him not to run around in his socks. She thought of how once he'd knocked his tooth out, and she'd sat him down and explained to him to not run or jump anymore.

And she thought of the shellac Dwight insisted on painting and repainting until the stairs were almost like liquid amber pouring down in a waterfall. And there he was at the top, standing in polyester socks.

She watched as one foot slipped, and as he went to catch himself but somehow couldn't let go of the letter to do so, the other foot stepped up to try to protect him and slipped again. And before she knew it, his feet were like a sled, and he was sliding down the stairs, tumbling, seesawing, coming down in great massive stops and poses, with a loud thumping. And he seemed to just let himself go as he cartwheeled downwards. Each time he cartwheeled, he'd smash his head against a step, leaving on the caramel waterfall droplets of a redder shellac. Down, down he fell until he landed at the bottom of the stairs at her feet.

She had screamed during his whole way down—

screamed his name. She had run forward and put her hands out as if to stop him from falling any further. As if she were going to stop a locomotive from running her over by pushing back the air in front of it. But her hands never even touched him.

He spun down and hit her legs, and she fell backwards too. There they were on the ground with her still screaming, then sitting up from her fallen position and crouching next to his bloodied head.

She screamed his name a few more times before running outside and calling the neighbors. She did the thing that she did every time anything happened—she called the neighbors like a child, because she knew they would be able to make the adult decisions that she could not make without their intervention or help.

Before running out, she pulled the letter out of Dwight's fingers, glancing at the drops of blood on the yellowing paper and seeing that the letter began: "My darling, my love. I don't know how much longer I cannot see you. I understand it is the first week that Dwight has come back, but I hate him for it, and I miss your smell. I miss your smile, your breasts, and your sloping back in my arms. I cannot sleep without you."

Dwight had found these letters and had read these words, and now he was very hurt. She realized that, once the neighbors helped him up, he would want an explanation.

When she came back with the neighbors, she left them with Dwight while she ran upstairs to her bedroom. She found the opened box and letters strewn everywhere in her closet. She put them all back into the box, put the lid back on, and hid it before grabbing towels and the first aid kit.

She ran back downstairs, where the man from next door was taking Dwight's pulse, while the woman called an ambulance on the phone in the hall. The neighbor put his hand out to stop her from trying to dab Dwight's shattered head with a towel. So she just stood there, holding the gauze and Band-Aids in silence.

She soon heard the ambulance's siren—she would hear it for the rest of her life, always somewhere on its way. She would always remember the neighbors coming in to help her clean up the messes she did not know how to fix, from burning popcorn to a destroyed husband. She sat in the hall and looked over at the living room that was dim and beautiful, looked at the paintings, the ones that Joe had helped her buy and the one that Joe himself had painted. She waited and waited, and she wondered where her life would go.

By the time the ambulance arrived, it was too late. Dwight was pronounced dead at the scene.

He was put on a stretcher and taken away. She did not need to explain anything. She simply told them that she had come home, called out, he'd come to the top of the stairs in his socks and simply tumbled down. They looked at his socks, and they looked at the shiny stairs, and they did not need any further explanation.

Dwight had been a slender man, a small man really, not the burly kind of fellow with muscular legs and large biceps who could've caught himself. Nothing like that. He simply fell down—a wisp of a man with a giant brain that seemed to pull him downwards with its weight, its contents spilling out at the bottom of the stairs at the feet of his cheating wife.

She sat in the hall in the chair next to the table below the mirror. She did not remember that chair ever being used by anyone, not even a salesman or deliveryman. It was a chair that simply sat in the hall as if in a waiting room, and she finally used it and finally understood what it was for. It was for when you did not know what room to go to and you did not know what to do next. It was for when you could not decide whether to stay in the house or run out screaming or simply lie down on the floor and wait to die.

She sat there until it got dark and the neighbors turned on the lights, and she could hear them fixing food in the kitchen while she sat there crying. The doctors had left her some pills to take, some kind of sedative. Jimmy was puttering around and soon would be ready for his bath, which the neighbors would also take care of. Luckily, he'd been next door when everything had happened and had no idea what was going on or why the neighbor's husband had been cleaning their hallway.

The neighbors made the phone calls to the family in Oklahoma and the colleagues at work.

Dwight's family made appropriate arrangements to come back for the funeral. She had none of this to worry about or deal with.

She picked up the telephone, telling the neighbors that she was calling the theater to let them know why she would not be coming in the next day. She called Joe instead and told him what had happened in the coolest, calmest voice that she could muster, without whimpering or crying for him to hold her. She simply explained that the neighbors were in the house and what had happened.

There was a silence on the other end of the line. She could hear Joe breathing, and she wondered if he was happy or if he was now troubled in the same way she was—with guilt, with fear of never having what it was they thought they wanted without any interruption or anyone to get in the way, but mostly with guilt.

She did not tell Joe exactly what happened since the neighbors were there. She said that she would stop by the theater in a few days to see everyone and tell them what had happened.

So the days went by, but she did not go to the theater as she had said she would. She simply sat with Jimmy and played with him and gave him her full and complete attention until two weeks had passed. Family had come and gone, burial arrangements were made, the funeral was held, where Dwight was mourned by his heartbroken colleagues. They were devastated that this great man, with a beautiful wife and young son, who had just come back from a war with medals and decorations, had died as he did. They looked at her wide red eyes and thought she'd waited so sweetly for him, and now he was gone again.

God's will seemed strange to them.

*

Joe had taken a chance by coming to see her at the house. After all, Dwight had been gone for only a few days. But they missed each other terribly, and she'd not been going to the theater very much in the first few weeks of Dwight's return.

Joe came around the back and knocked on the kitchen door.

She stepped outside, afraid to even invite him in. She saw him in the garden, suddenly seeing his unusual good looks among the familiar things of her back porch. He seemed even more appealing than he was in his own environment. He seemed to be a dangerous presence at her house, and she sat on the steps of the back door as he squatted before her and held her hands in his. They simply looked at each other as tears ran down her face.

Little Jimmy was in the kitchen. She had shut the door so that he could not come out and see that she had company. His little hands could not quite reach the doorknob, so he banged on the door a few times. She turned and said, "Jimmy, play with your toys for a minute, and I'll be right in."

They sat quietly on the step for a while, saying nothing in particular. She asked how it was going at the theater and then showed him the bougainvillea that was blooming. She showed him the dew on the leaves as if he were a child and had never seen such a thing before. He looked at her things around her—at the wicker basket with her gardening gloves—and he saw her in her own world, as a wife and mother.

Even though he'd been to the house before, it had never been during the household's natural state. It had been during the times she had thrown parties and changed the place and herself for her new friends. He had never been in that squatting position in the backyard seeing her wearing her housecoat.

And even when he had been there alone with her late at night before Dwight's return, it had been as if they were both sneaking around a house that was not either one of theirs. She'd been in her theater-type outfits, and he had come in furtively, both of them whispering like intruders. Now that he had surprised her in her everyday environment, he finally saw that this was where she really lived. He saw that Jimmy was really her son—not a child in her care who she would leave with the neighbors when she had to be somewhere else. He heard the child crying "Mommy, Mommy," and he fully understood that she was a wife and mother living in her house, but that she longed to be someone else.

Joe's heart sank. In that moment he knew he

would have to let her go. Simultaneously she was thinking that he had come for her and that his surprising her at the back door and taking such a risk was actually a sign. Perhaps the next time he would load her and little Jimmy up in the car, and they would run away together. She would look back on that day and find it amazing that their thoughts had been so different from one another's, based on the very same experience of sitting on the steps and all the rest that came in the minutes that followed.

It was silent for a few minutes save for the chirping of birds. And then there was the shrill warbling scream from inside the house. Their shoulders stiffened, and they both knew that something really bad had happened to Jimmy. They ran inside through the kitchen, down the hall to where the stairs were just in time to see Jimmy coming around from inside the living room, his face and the front of his little shirt covered in red. His hands covering his mouth were coated in his own syrupy bright blood.

When Jimmy saw Joe, he was startled since he hadn't realized that his mother was outside with someone else, and this frightened him again, so he began to scream some more. Joe realized what was happening, and this made the situation even worse— the unnaturalness of it.

The child had somehow fallen and hurt his mouth, and she felt crushed about what she had been doing while he was smashing his face.

They both ran to him, but he turned and ran away, looking fearfully at Joe. She asked Joe to stay back, went after the boy, and picked him up. She looked at his face and asked him what happened. He could not answer because he was shaking, and his mouth was gurgling with blood. She saw that one of his baby teeth in the front was missing, and of course, his being so little, it was too soon for it to have fallen out naturally. It must've been knocked out. She told Joe to look for the tooth, and he ran into the living room.

She asked Jimmy, "Did you fall?" He nodded. She asked him, "Were you bouncing on the couch like I asked you not to?" He nodded again. She held him and said, "There, there, we'll figure it out."

Joe came into the hallway from the living room, holding a bloody tooth. There was a trail of blood from where Jimmy had fallen face-first into the heavy coffee table.

She felt like someone whispered in her ear, told her what to say next, and so she said, "I think we put the tooth in some milk then put it back into his gum." Joe ran to the kitchen, opened the icebox, and poured a glass of milk, dropping the tooth into it. She followed him to the kitchen with Jimmy in her arms and reached into the glass, not wanting Joe to put his big fingers in Jimmy's little mouth since the boy cowered when he came near him anyway.

She took out the little tooth from the glass of milk and put it into the hole where it had been. Jimmy began to shriek at the top of his lungs as she put her thumb underneath the tooth and shoved upwards. As the tooth went back in with a crunch, the child turned red and began to arch his back in her arms. He was kicking, and tears were practically flying horizontally from his eyes.

She knew that the neighbors would be able to hear the screaming, so she turned to Joe and said, "You'd better go. I'll take care of this."

He left, and that was the last time she would see him. In his letters, he would promise to keep coming, but he never did.

She picked up little Jimmy and walked next door to the neighbors' house just as they were on their way over to her. One of them, having glimpsed Joe leaving, assumed the worst but said nothing. The neighbor told her the baby tooth could not be saved and reinserted. Only adult teeth could, so they would have to pull little Jimmy's tooth back out again.

Her heart sank. Jimmy had calmed down in their arms, as he always did.

And soon, when the neighbors moved back to the Midwestern state they were from, they would take little Jimmy with them at her suggestion and keep him as their own—as they felt they deserved.

She sat and watched them, realizing for the first time how much they loved her son and how completely comfortable he was with them. Her mind was with Joe again. The neighbor lady gripped the tooth with one thumb and forefinger and yanked it out. Little Jimmy felt the pain all over again and screamed. This time, because he was in the neighbor's arms, he was able to make desperate eye contact with her as he cried. But she looked through the child.

She knew that she wouldn't see Joe or run away with him. She knew he was gone for good, and she knew that his letters would be all that she would have.

She would be sealed tightly into her marriage to Dwight.

*

She wasn't exactly sure of the full details of just what Dwight's work was after he came home. He'd been doing it for a brief time. She knew it had something to do with fuel, but that somehow he had become interested in wolves. This was strange, since he was an engineer. But somehow he had gotten in with some scientists while studying the raw fuel in Alaska and discovered that they were working with wolves. This fascinated him, so he kept in touch with them and would tell her about their research.

He told her that wolves were becoming extinct in certain areas and that on Coronation Island in Alaska they were doing an experiment where they were going to release two female and two male wolves, shoot a couple of the deer, which already populated the small forty-five-square-mile island, so that the wolves would have something to eat, and then check up on them in a year to see if they made it and if they had begun to populate the island.

This seemed rather insane to her. Why put the wolves there and why kill the deer for them instead of letting them catch them themselves? But she realized as Dwight explained it to her that the wolves needed to know that there were deer around the island, so a little help from the scientists would get them going.

The first she heard about the experiment was about six months after they had gone back and found wolf tracks and droppings. In them, they had found the remains of deer. The deer population had moved up the hill to protect itself from the wolves. But still the wolves were alive and well and feeding on the deer, and the deer were running from the wolves on a forty-five-square-mile island.

She did not find this encouraging for some reason. Something about it seemed strange. And then a few months later, Dwight told her that something odd had happened. That they had gone on the island and found that the wolf population had decreased and the droppings they found contained very few deer remains and far more wolf remains instead. Meaning the wolves were eating each other.

When she heard this, something inside her shuddered—she wasn't sure what. She felt a terrible fear and started thinking about the wolves growing hungry as the clever deer that were used to the terrain moved up the hills. The wolves, who didn't know why they'd been put there, had grown confused and hungry. She pictured them seeing one of their cubs die and, after loving it and mourning, deciding it was time to eat it.

She thought about little Jimmy. She looked at him, at his fleshy little arm, thought about food and what she might be willing to do if she was hungry enough. She playfully bit Jimmy's arm a little too hard and saw the quick pain and then fear in his eyes followed by relief when she stopped. He was wild enough to understand that it was not entirely unlikely that he might be eaten by the bigger animals in charge of him.

The whole wolf thing drove her crazy. It was years later when she went through Dwight's papers that she learned about the final phase of what had happened on Coronation Island. Years and years later, long after Dwight had died, she discovered that the wolves had died out entirely and never recovered after the cannibalism. The deer population had gone back to normal. Putting the wolves where they did not belong had hurt them even more than if they had let them dwindle and then adapt in their natural habitats.

It would have taken a much, much larger space for both deer and wolf to survive in an experiment anyway. That the deer had made it and the wolves had not was strange because of the wolves' aggression and the deer's timidity. Somehow the deer reproduced more or perhaps just played a better defensive game.

Planting wolves seemed like a stupid thing to do. They called it "planting," as though they were placing evidence of wrongdoing to frame somebody for a crime. Or burying it in the ground like seeds.

The government would plant them too close to property lines and ranches in their efforts to preserve wildlife. But the ranchers would wake up and find all their chickens ravaged by the nighttime visitors. It was madness. The predator wolves only did what they had to in order to live and feed their cubs.

They were not crazy killers or a real menace. They were just out of place and kept doing what they did according to their own customs.

*

She rarely understood that it was happening when it was happening, but once in a while after a big spell of it she knew exactly what it was, and in some ways, her concerns were not about herself but about how worried the thing made everybody else.

When she had one of her spells, she would go into it, and it would be entirely absorbing. It was like a waking dream. She would slip into one particular place in her mind and would look around and recognize where she was, and it would be a place where she had been as a child, or it would be a scene in her life as a young woman or a conversation she might have had or may have hoped that she would eventually have with someone, to sort things out or just talk.

However, when she was not in "time travel," as she called it, she knew that she was living these imaginary moments while her actual body was wherever it was—at its real age and around her current acquaintances, who probably were not very clear about what was happening to her.

They were dealing with a sleepwalker, and it was their alarmed concern that made her so sad.

She didn't suffer at the beginning phase of the disease. She felt it was actually quite dreamy. She was entertained almost all the time. She was going through her life, every minute of it, from the time she was born all the way until now. Finishing up unfinished business in almost every decade and practically in every week.

But, knowing enough about Alzheimer's, she also knew that things would get bad and it wouldn't be a dreamy bit of time travel for long. The symptoms would become physical, and her emotions could turn the whole thing into a nightmare, and then the fears of the people who were around her would come true. They would be stuck taking care of someone who was dying and whose body had completely given up.

But as it was, she was in that dreamy place. If only the disease could simply let her stay there. If only she could simply live her life over and over.

She had no control over exactly what dream she would have or whom she would bump into again after all this time or whom she would mistake for somebody else, and that was part of the fun of it. She really didn't know if her brain had any order and reason for doing what it did, so she simply went along for the ride.

The one person who seemed quite at ease with this was the home nurse who stayed in the house with her. When she found herself going into a spell, the nurse would not be upset or worried.

When she'd mistaken her for all kinds of different people and had thought all kinds of different people were in the room with them, the nurse had simply played along. It was as if she was able to travel with her. She'd ask, "Who are you talking to?"

And Mrs. Randall would simply say, "Joe is here, and so is Jimmy, and as you can see Jim's lost a tooth, and his gums are bleeding. He hit his head on the coffee table, his mouth, in fact, and Joe and I were outside and are figuring out what to do. Now you don't know what to do, do you, nurse?"

"Yes, I do. I think you can soak the tooth in milk and clean it off and just pop it right back in."

"Oh, what a great idea!" she responded. She had followed the nurse's direction and had told Joe that's what you did and that it would work. In some ways, she had always wondered where she got that idea about the milk and the tooth, and now she knew that perhaps the nurse had told her all along. Perhaps the nurse's voice from the future had gotten into her brain and given her the idea. Perhaps Alzheimer's worked both ways, and now she could figure out where all the little thoughts throughout her life had come from. Maybe they'd come from the future while she was reliving the past.

So she began to wonder about that some more when she wasn't deep in her dreams, and the nurse would discuss the past with her. She told her about her husband's stories about planting wolves and everything that her husband had told her about the experiment on Coronation Island. The nurse had thought that it was really quite sad, like displacing a people and wondering why they didn't get along and why they started infighting and having wars. The nurse thought cannibalism was an extreme form of self-destruction—turning on one's own people was just a very carnal, very basic symbol of grief.

Mrs. Randall had been impressed with the nurse's abstract thinking. As she felt herself slipping back into that dream again and Dwight told her all about planting wolves, she kept in mind what it was that the nurse had told her, and she told Dwight exactly what it was the nurse had said.

Dwight's head had snapped up, and he'd looked at her and said, "My God, you're right."

She wanted to tell Dwight how he would die and about Alzheimer's being time travel, that she was an old woman now. But throughout the ages, there had been so many warnings about changing the outcome of things by changing the past that she was too afraid to.

She was pouring tea in the yellow cups that she loved so much. She placed a cup in front of the nurse in the living room. The nurse was enchanted by the paintings. She stood by the fire and stared up at them over and over again, as if seeing something new each time just as Mrs. Randall did each time she visited the scenes of her life. She'd suddenly noticed that the cat had been in the hall too when Jimmy's tooth was bleeding.

She told the nurse about her thoughts—about how she was aware of her Alzheimer's and how she was simply going back and running around in time like a spaceman. That she was taking as much from the present into the past as she was bringing of the past into the present, and she was wondering if that perhaps she was able to affect the past as if it wasn't just a dream but really was going back in time. That sort of thing.

The nurse looked at her first, and she could tell that she was wondering if this was some other stage of senility. Another wave of thoughts passed behind the nurse's eyes, though, a wave of understanding and comprehension. She sat up straight and alert and replied:

"Oh, my goodness!"

Clearly, she understood completely, and they both nodded and thought. There was a hush. The nurse picked up her cup and drank thoughtfully, looked at Mrs. Randall, and said:

"You know what I think, Mrs. Randall? I think you really are time traveling. I don't see this as an impossibility, and I don't see how anyone could disprove that."

Mrs. Randall knew that she had chosen that nurse for a reason, and she knew that she had told the right person. Perhaps she could help her process these travels through time and throughout her own life. There were times when, after going back to a certain era and maybe taking back something from the present or maybe having a conversation she meant to have, that she wished someone could be there to hear about her adventure when she got back to real time. About how she'd been going and fixing things that had up to then bothered her or had sat in the back of her mind. Little things like never having thanked someone or never having bought a dress.

It was almost as if, by going back and changing these things, she was unburdening her brain of the weight of them. She was making corrections to her own chronology, and the nurse was allowing her to. The nurse was not telling her that she was wrong or crazy. She was saying, "Yes, I agree with you."

This was exactly what was happening in reality. Mrs. Randall couldn't believe that no one had seen dementia this way before.

The sun began to set, and they sat and looked at the paintings in the changing light. They sat on the couch and waited until the room was pitch-black, but the nurse and Mrs. Randall didn't move and just kept staring at the fire together for what seemed like hours until the last ember glowed and then disappeared.

*

Dwight was reading the paper while he ate breakfast as he did every morning. He had just smashed the tines of his fork into the yolk of his eggs and was dipping in some bacon as he turned the page of his newspaper. He thought about little else but his breakfast and the news.

She watched him a little while standing at the sink. She was washing a glass and looking out at the garden, and she would look over her shoulder ever so slightly to look at him. She would wonder what it was like to be him. To be so present for what it was that he was doing rather than in his head. Or maybe he was in his head, and she just couldn't know. But she would look at him, and she would look at their son Jimmy as he sat on the floor and quietly played, and she would wonder what they were thinking. Jimmy was such a good child and seemed entirely engrossed in his toy but didn't look entirely satisfied with it. Perhaps that is how she herself seemed.

She kept washing and rewashing the glass—it seemed as if she was very much in the flow of that activity, but her head, of course, was filled with all kinds of other things.

She turned around after putting the glass in the dish rack and wiped her hands across the top of her apron. She gave a little cough and faked clearing her throat.

Dwight looked up briefly and smiled at her, then looked back down at his paper. Then, realizing he was done, he folded it carefully and put it to the side and began to drink his orange juice and take a bite of his buttered toast. He looked up at her again and smiled again.

He was indeed a nice man and a good husband, so he was unable to understand why she felt a deep dissatisfaction with him and sometimes even anger as if he was withholding a whole other world of things that would make her feel good.

She decided to ask him about this. She decided to have a real conversation with him. Without being frightened she had the thought that perhaps she could bring home some of the things that she had or thought she had with Joe—bring that same excitement to Dwight. It was as if she had caught this bug of art, and talking, sharing, and dreaming were a part of that bug. Dwight just hadn't caught it yet. Maybe she could give it to him, it could become theirs, and she could stay in her marriage and be happy in it instead of daydreaming about Joe at the window.

Joe, while she did the dishes. Joe, while she bathed Jimmy. Joe, while she sat on the couch in the summertime and wondered about dusting and dinner.

Joe was not at the theater, having gone south for a family funeral, and certainly after Jimmy had fallen and knocked out his teeth, she had known he'd go away. The letters still came, though. The long love letters that kept her in a state. He sent them to the theater, and she read them in her closet when she got home.

At first, she thought that Joe had taken that passionate feeling with him when he left, but after some thought, she realized that half of that feeling was her own. He only took away his half. And perhaps she could share that half with Dwight and in some way inspire another half inside him, making a whole in her own home and with her own husband.

All she had to do was to broach it with him like a stranger instead of assuming things about him that she knew weren't necessarily true. She was being very optimistic as she looked at Dwight for a moment, looked at how close he was to finishing his breakfast, and she decided to take the opportunity before he was gone into his own world.

"Dwight?"

"Yes, dear?"

"I was wondering...what are your dreams? What I mean to say is, not your night dreams, not what your brain does when you're asleep, but what are your dreams for this life?"

"Do you mean my goals for the future?"

"Something like that."

"Darling, you really don't have to worry about these things. I plan on continuing to work and to provide for you and to pay off the house—we're very close to that. I'll keep working on this cold steam energy thing I've been doing and really plan for our retirement—our future. And maybe for a new child— well, not to say that Jimmy's old news! He certainly has a worn-out look! We can be a growing family.

"Are you thinking about redecorating? Is that why you're asking? Because I think that we could perhaps afford that in a few months. If you wanted some new chairs or paint, you could get that now. I thought you were busy with the garden and, anyway, well…my dreams are our dreams. To be a good family and, you know, the holidays are coming and that sort of thing…. Celebrating, being at home with you."

She was so focused on her own point that it blinded her to how sweetly he was gazing at her as he said all that. She replied with great disappointment.

"Oh, I see. That isn't exactly what I meant but, oh, maybe it is. I guess what I was thinking was, I just wondered if you ever thought about maybe doing things that you didn't get to do every day. What if you had some secret dreams like being a singer or learning to dance? I don't know."

"Now I can't say that I think about being a singer or want anything that I don't have. I'm very happy with my life. Do you want me to ask you what your dreams are?"

"I guess I do. Yes, yes. I think I'd like to tell you about mine."

"Well, I'm certainly interested. I don't have to leave for another ten minutes."

"Well, I was thinking I'd like to go to Morocco and really travel, and how maybe after volunteering so much at the theater while you were gone.... I just really got to thinking, perhaps I could take some acting lessons and maybe try out for a small part in a play or film. Or maybe I could do a little more seamstress work. Or not. Maybe just travel. I was thinking about Turkey or Egypt. There are so many places in the world to go. We went to Paris and everything, but there's so much more to the world than Europe. But a job might be a good thing, and the acting class or some other classes. So I could really just explore myself. Learn about different religions. And I would certainly like to study some of them and find out what people's concept of the spirit world is and that sort of thing."

Dwight stared blankly but was aware enough of his face to try and be polite. He looked at his wife, and he wondered when she had become so unhappy with their lives—when she had become so dissatisfied. His heart sagged. He wanted to give her everything that she wanted so urgently, but he could not give her the things that were in the dreams she shared with him at that moment.

What surprised him was the astonishing level of shame he felt, shame at himself that weighed his head and made him look down at his plate.

The yellow smears that were left over from his eggs colored the shame he felt when he thought about how satisfied he'd been a moment ago and the stupidity that came with realizing that someone right there with him had dreams that went so far beyond who he was, at that table shoveling breakfast into his mouth.

He felt deeply embarrassed about how unsatisfactory it must be for someone with such dreams to sit in the kitchen with him in the morning eating eggs.

He wanted to tell this to her, but, of course, that was not appropriate or possible. It had not occurred to him or any man of his generation to share the feelings inside them when their women complained or talked about things they didn't have, which translated to complaint for the man who heard those words.

And because they never told the women about how they heard things, the women were never able to, in turn, let them know that what they were doing was not complaining but sharing dreams and hoping that perhaps the husband would join them in their fantasy.

And so, the men and women went on in their mutual confusion, living together, occasionally one of them expressing how it would be better if things were different while all the other heard was that they were inadequate.

Eventually, walls were built to protect their

hearts.

Dwight stood and took his plate to the sink, ran some water over the egg before it dried and would be too difficult for his wife to wash. He put his hands gently on her shoulders and, without being able to make eye contact, kissed her on the cheek and smiled and nodded and said have a good day, dear, and I will see you tonight.

He walked down the hall and grabbed his jacket and briefcase. He didn't stop for anything else, barely slowing down, and headed straight out the front door to his car.

Had he been a child or a woman, he would have been sobbing by the time he reached the front seat, but he wasn't. He put it all into his heart. He put it all inside and let it sit there without looking at it again.

She watched him leave as if she had not spoken the things she had said. He didn't even acknowledge a single thing or ask any follow-up questions. He simply ignored her as if she were a buzzing fly in the room or a child gibbering about nothing. And some last fading bit of loyalty to their marriage and to Dwight got squashed in a moment, and her sense of survival kicked in. It was a matter of survival for her to be allowed to dream and for her to have someone to engage in those dreams with her and to help her pursue them—she was sure of that.

Dwight, as it seemed to her in that moment, had simply put his hand on the top of her head and pushed her down under water so that she would stop saying all the things he did not want to hear.

*

It had taken almost four decades to get over the intoxication of the nights that Mrs. Randall spent sitting in her garden with its high walls and hedges, never certain that the neighbors could not see. Or the nights she spent with Joe chatting quietly, knowing that perhaps people could hear them, but not caring that much.

It had taken her many years to get over it, because it had taken her many years to stop chasing the high. The high of sitting at dusk with leaves all around and clay tiles under her feet, wearing sandals the way she used to—with toenail polish darker than usual and perhaps darker than was decent—with Joe gently hooking his finger around her toe and then letting it go again.

It was before they'd become lovers, so every touch was electric. And about another two decades of yearning and searching for those nights' special feeling with the Santa Ana winds and the moon overhead and the closeness of his breath while they talked.

It was a trick that took two decades to be discovered, that so much of what she missed about him, so much of what she yearned for, perhaps had to do with the wine and the tobacco.

She'd never drank before, the way she did with

Joe. She had always sipped and focused on the taste and had no real use for the heaviness that alcohol brought with it. It had simply made her feel uncomfortable with the people she was around to suddenly not have all her bearings and not have all her inhibitions in place. It had felt wrong, so she had avoided it.

But with Joe in the garden and with the conversations they would have, along with the long puffs of cigarettes, the wine was different. It was in a new context. She wanted her inhibitions to disappear, and somehow it was as if the more she drank the wine, the more she was able to hear what he was saying. He would be telling her about the fourth wall in theater or about Matisse and Modigliani or he would be telling her about what Ischia was like in August or all the other places he had been to.

But mostly how he would tell her who he believed she was. It was the act of him telling her who she was that was the greatest intoxicant. Up until then, she had not known and had not thought she would like the person she would find, even if she knew. It was the revelation of what this man saw when he looked at her that was the greatest drunk of all.

She could still close her eyes and smell the old flowers if she went outside at night. Even though she had kicked the chase for the tobacco and wine of the distant past, if she smelled the flowers while her eyes were closed and put her two fingers up against her lips as if the cigarette was in them and breathed it in, it all came back.

She used to suck the smoke past her tongue, down her throat, calming her shoulders back down away from her sides and away from her ears. Blowing out the smoke and squinting a little until the orange curl of her own hair hanging in her eyes seemed like something separate from her—perhaps a leaf from a tree. And she'd just be listening with her whole self.

She would be hearing Joe's voice as if it was part of the things that happened outside—the birds, the squirrels, all the little noises around her, and the round womb of the wineglass in her hands, all warm. The darkness of the wine as it came up to her lips where she'd take a huge gulp. She could gulp it without worrying about being ladylike. She'd let it stay in her mouth, her cheeks a little puffed out, and then slowly let it trickle down her throat.

The instant warmth and slight alarm of it hitting her stomach, and then the peace that followed and the dictionary of new meanings that were suddenly available through the alcohol, were what made the chase last for so long. How words had different undertones than she usually thought they did, with multiple meanings and arrangements. The words would come out of her own mouth, even.

Long after Joe had gone, she had tried to find this magical portal through wine and tobacco in the backyard by herself, but it was gone. She had tried and tried, but not having the alcoholic gene in her body, she had known to eventually give up the attempts and stay watchful for other vehicles of transcendence.

But the nights in the garden had been a time and place that made every other time and place seem small and meaningless.

There was something to be said for not having too good a time. Maybe you don't want one event to be so amazing, so good, so right, that it makes every other thing in your life fall backwards and seem small.

And even if you do have such an experience, maybe it should never be attached to one person, making them the focal point. Maybe you just don't want to have such a good time.

Joe would run his thick fingers down the side of her face. He would press his thumb against her lips, and it was there that he kissed her for the first time.

It had been like an atom bomb had dropped on her head. She went crazy. It was as if her body was about to give up all control of itself. She had never experienced such a thing and almost felt unwell.

In one small movement, Joe was able to take her entire moral compass and belief system and turn it on its ear.

He'd shaken it up in a way that she didn't think it could be shaken any further, having already found herself in the garden alone with other men, herself being a married woman. What could be more naughty than that? She didn't think that it could go any further than that, simply because she hadn't imagined it would. She didn't think that she could go any wilder inside, but his lips against hers made her go as far as a person could go away from what they thought they were.

She had been ruined.

*

Mrs. Randall watched the parade of motorcycles go by on Verdugo Road, past the park and college. They were moving slowly. It was a big procession. They were heading away towards another part of the city and then out of town towards wherever it was they were going to have whatever sort of fundraiser they were having to benefit whatever charity it was that they seemed so dramatically to be championing.

She saw him slowly rolling towards her. He was not wearing a helmet, which she knew was probably against the law in this day and age, not like in her day when you could do whatever you wanted and wear a soft scarf on your head and go a hundred miles an hour. Of course, nothing could really go a hundred miles an hour back then. But she saw him coming, and she saw the sun glisten off his strawberry blond hair.

He was a ginger boy, and he had freckles—she could tell he had tried to tan away his true coloring, perhaps not on purpose, but certainly if he had not been tanned the freckles would've been an amazing array of rusts and bright colors over white, white skin. He had the red-rimmed eyes of real redheads and the bright blue glistening irises fringed by the blond eyelashes, which he'd perhaps had darkened, as she knew people did.

She would get the free local circular with all the ads for all these things in them—eyelash tinting, freckle bleaching, hair dynamiting—all of the things people did now.

But he could not hide that he was a ginger cat on a motorcycle coming towards her with a slight bump on the nose that looked like it should have been a bigger bump but wasn't. She saw he had chapped-looking lips, which weren't chapped at all but simply looked that way because they were the same color as the rest of his face before it had tanned. The untanned pink lips turned up in a smile when he caught her watching him approach, and the smile became toothy, and she was amazed by the teeth.

He had the bright white teeth of a cartoon creature. They were not the teeth of an Irish boy or whatever it was that this man was. They were the teeth of somebody else. Bright, bright light bulbs dangling all crushed together under the bright blue of his eyes.

He smiled, his eyes twinkled, and he looked at her in a way that he should've saved for a younger woman. But she took the look on anyhow.

She could tell he was a movie star or something, because she didn't believe real people looked at each other that way, or maybe they did and maybe somehow in this light he had mistaken her for someone his own age, and so he was giving her that look. That look that was oh-so-sly and made her smile right back.

The motorcycle rolled by, and he gave a little nod and a little wink all at once. It was certainly nervy and very cheeky, and she gave a little wink and a smile back although she didn't know how to wink and wondered how it looked with the wrinkles around her eyes. It probably simply looked like a squint, and she was relieved she wasn't good at winking. But she couldn't believe she was even trying to.

He went by and waved his hand. It was in one of those fingerless leather gloves. His fingernails, manicured the color of a pale petal and perfect, looked like those of a young girl going to her first dance.

This was a boy from farm stock or some kind of country background, and he had been taken out and away. His people were from where they were supposed to be, but the invention of roads and planes—all the things that made it possible for people to go away from where they came from took him to places where his skin had to be changed. And here he was now, no longer out pushing a plough or doing what it was his ancestors had done in order to have such thick necks and big fingers, or to be so freckled and ginger all over.

Mrs. Randall felt quite lucid that day—lucid enough to go to the park, and to smile and see what was going on and understand it fully. In spite of her common sense, she let the boy on the motorcycle catch her eye. He couldn't have been more than forty, and she laughed about it with a good, good feeling.

She thought that perhaps it was like some strange virus that lay dormant in you so that once you'd been seduced by the wrong kind of person—just once in your life—and tasted what it was like to be giddy with it, you would always be a little bit susceptible to other wrong kinds of men.

The actor who went by reminded her of a modern, strange version of all the actors she had seen and known to stay away from at the Alex Theatre. By the time she met her sturdy Joe, she had had situations with a few other men, and she knew the caliber of their seduction was dangerous beyond anything she could afford.

And yet here it was, decades later—this new version of that same danger.

The new version of that astonishingly delicious insincerity.

Chapter Three •

Rodney

RODNEY HAD FIRST NOTICED the bleeding during preproduction. He had thought that perhaps he'd leaned his hand on the edge of a table with a loose nail or tack, and that was why his palm had that dot of blood right in its center. But by the end of the first day, when the little dot of blood had appeared on his right palm, the other dot of blood appeared on his left palm and then right on top of both his hands as if the dots had seeped right through to the other sides.

It was early July in Los Angeles, and once a few people noticed the blood coming through the Band-Aids and then the gauze wrapping, Rodney was forced to wear work gloves to hide the growing dots of blood. But TV preproduction for a production assistant was a week of copying schedules, making calls, and picking up various office supplies for the shoot. Nothing that needed work gloves, so it was difficult to explain away the gloves as a grip or an electrician might have.

And then there was the heat. It was a hot summer already, and Rodney's dark complexion sucked up the rays, and his tall stature made him feel even closer to the sun, so the gloves drove him to an itchy, damp distraction.

Finally, John noticed and made fun of him a little bit. Usually, when his cousin John did that, it would have made him give some explanation for whatever he was being mocked for, and he would have somehow changed his behavior out of embarrassment. But now Rodney said nothing and did nothing in response to the ribbing until John had to stop him in the hallway outside the office and ask.

"Rod, what's with the gloves?"

"Listen, man. You're not gonna believe this. It's just ridiculous and kind of gross and I don't want to upset the females in the office. It's just that my hands are bleeding."

"Your what?"

"My hands are bleeding."

"So, go to the goddamn medic, Rodney! Jesus Christ!"

"Yeah, well, it's nothing I can explain. Nothing happened to them! I think I need to get a whole checkup, and I don't have the insurance yet. And I'm just now catching up on the bills for the lung thing."

"Rodney, you are a man with one lung, and you need to take care of your health because you breathe harder than other people, and every little thing can be tougher on your body. You need to take care of this hand thing because you don't want to seem like a fucking nut and lose this job I got you, man."

"I know, I know."

"Let me see."

"What?"

"The cuts or whatever. Take off the gloves and tell me what you punched your hands through. Let me see."

"I didn't punch anything."

"Take off the goddamn gloves, Rodney—I can't fuck around and kid with you. Let me see, and let's get you to the goddamned studio medic and take care of this before you make a fool of me."

Rodney pulled off one glove at a time, immediately revealing the now nickel-sized bloodspots that were already soaking through the new gauze he had wrapped just an hour earlier. John winced at his cousin's hands, and then his face went blank as Rodney flipped his palms back and forth to show the matching spots on the fronts of each hand. John grabbed Rodney by the arm, and they both instinctively knew to shuffle sideways right into the men's room down the hall and quickly step into a stall, which they locked behind them.

Rodney unraveled the gauze, not knowing how much deeper the wounds had become since he last dared to look. There was a tiled hush in the bathroom stall. They could hear the rhythmic drip of a faucet and some distant muffled walkie-talkie sounds from the back lot, where there was another television show shooting its first episode, just as they were about to.

John's eyes met Rodney's briefly as he raised his

hands up between them and rotated them to show the full scope of the wounds. Blood oozed darkly and steadily from both sides of each wound, and the openings looked like the insides of a small cone, as if whatever had made the punctures had been beveled. The punctures went all the way through each hand. John's mouth fell open.

"What the fuck did you do to your hands, Rodney?"

"I swear to god, John, I didn't do anything.... I'm not crazy.... I know how hard it is to get into show business.... I wouldn't fuck with your AD gig.... I wouldn't do anything to screw this up for myself.... I just woke up last week, and there were little dots, and then they kept growing and it doesn't hurt or anything but it won't stop bleeding, and I don't have a fever like when I had the lung infection.... There is nothing else wrong.... I just got holes in my hands!"

"Like Jesus fucking Christ? Is that what you're telling me?"

"No! I don't know, man—I'm just scared and need to hide it so I can just do my goddamn job."

"Wrap it up and put on the gloves and let me think. Jesus fucking Christ, Rodney. This is fucking insane. We have nine months of shooting to do, and I can't start the first week with you fucking running around telling people you're my family and showing them your hands.... Just wrap them up and let me think. Now let's get back to work and act normal."

And so they did. But they didn't come up with any ideas, and the weeks and months rolled on with Rodney working right into production on the soundstage with his gauze and gloves, and like most idiosyncrasies on a shooting crew in Los Angeles, even the oddest habits and choices of attire—gloves or otherwise—are eventually accepted and finally forgotten.

It is not in the least bit difficult to hide one's stigmata on the set of an episodic television show.

*

Rodney had been driving for what seemed like hours. He'd been stuck in traffic and really didn't see any way out of it. He still had lots of pickups and drop-offs—it was madness.

The gloves were burning up his hands. His hands were sweating from the heat of the sun beating through the car windows down on the dark fabric of his gloves and the gauze underneath.

Some days, when he was stuck in traffic, he would just start to cry. He would let himself go and let the tears rush down his cheeks.

This would happen mostly if he'd been listening to talk radio and especially if he was able to find some sort of religious show on the AM stations, somebody talking tender and kind, somebody nice. Public radio people saying nice things, saying nice things gently, would make him cry. So different from work—so different from the real world—it just made him cry. Made him feel safe enough to cry and wonder when the bleeding would stop. When his hands would go back to normal.

His cousin, John, wasn't too happy about the bleeding hands and didn't want to speculate about them, nor did he want anyone knowing. He'd gotten Rodney the job on the show and didn't want to look bad.

Rodney felt like he was starting to really lose his mind. He never realized how much his hands meant to him. How important it was to have them be bare and able to breathe. Almost like they were flowers and needed light and air and water. Having a wound like that on your hands—the very things you feel the world with—it was too much.

It was getting to him, he thought, and yet he couldn't go nuts because there was no time for that.

So he sat at La Brea and Santa Monica and looked at the mall across the street. The outdoor mall where you could see some of the people sitting outside in the coffee shop. He wondered why anyone would want to sit anywhere near the street with all the traffic and drink their coffee. How could that possibly be relaxing for them, knowing that people were trapped in their cars while they sat outside and drank their coffee? But they did, and so he watched them out there in the free air and wondered what sort of work they did to let them take a coffee break at four in the afternoon. Not just one where they drank some of the office coffee in the hallway, but one where they actually left their office and went and sat down outside.

Even though he wasn't in his office, he was definitely working. He certainly wasn't lounging around anywhere. He wanted to know about the kind of work where you really care, where you bust your ass the same way he did at his job but you were proud and happy at the end of it. He suddenly felt stupid because he believed that doctors had that kind of work. But stupid people couldn't be doctors, so they had shitty jobs.

He had always assumed it might be fun to work in show business, because it just seemed so glamorous and exciting, but he'd found that it wasn't really all that different from construction. Being in production was strange because at the end of the day you didn't know what to be proud of.

He felt confused and lost about it and just wanted to sleep, but all he did was dream about work and dream about all the voices and the sound of the walkie-talkie in his ear.

Somehow, once you were in showbiz, you couldn't get out. It had once made him feel really special that everyone called on him for everything. He was starting to think that the "special" wasn't in a good way—but in a way that he'd become so useless in every other part of his life that work was the only place where he was valuable. He wondered, if he gave it up now, what the hell would he do with himself? It paid well, and a job is a job. He knew he had a job that everyone else in LA wanted to do, but it still felt like being in a dream all by himself all day long.

Rodney looked at his hands and realized that the steering wheel was wet. He looked at his gloves—the blood had seeped through the gauze, through the lining, and through the thick gloves onto the blackness of the plastic steering wheel. Then a drop of it fell down and hit him on his knee. Luckily, he was wearing shorts, so there was nothing to stain but his own skin. His own deep skin with the blood on top of it looking a little bit like raspberry sauce.

He pulled over and rested his head on the steering wheel, then looked around for a sporting goods store or drugstore or something. He'd have to start over—buy yet another pair of gloves and more gauze. Clean and rewrap, even though the wound seemed to never infect no matter how dirty he let it get. It just seeped blood, and in the past week, it had gotten so you could see right through it to the other side. He just couldn't bear to tell anyone, it was so crazy. He imagined they might put him in a cage at a science school, or maybe the government would kidnap him.

In his imagination, it was never good. It was always bad, and every scenario ended with there being hard cold proof that he was a freak and not like anybody else, and that would be the end of that.

So he found a drugstore, pulled into the back parking lot, and headed in quickly, thinking, "Jesus Christ.... If I am the Messiah, shouldn't I be doing something more important than changing the bandages on my hands and picking up Xerox ink and jet ink for the copier and picking up lunch for actors and tampons for producers and gifts for that fool's wife? Is this my purpose?"

One of Rodney's job descriptions was to take care of Chris Campari's every whim. It was not as difficult as it sounded. Chris Campari did not have too many unusual whims. He was quite predictable. He had a steady stream of repetitive whims. The same stuff over and over again in rotation, and Rodney loved to do these things for him because Rodney loved Chris Campari. And Chris Campari loved Chris Campari, and he even loved Rodney a little.

Chris Campari liked his coffee a certain way from Starbucks, and he wanted it around the same time every day. Chris Campari liked to occasionally go to strip clubs. During times of stress, this would be more than occasionally and sometimes just ever so slightly more complicated than simply going to the strip club and leaving again.

Chris was always on some sort of diet, and even though the diet changed, Chris did not change in relation to dieting. He would discuss at length or rather talk at length at Rodney, thinking that Rodney was somehow responding, about what he wanted from his body and why this diet was the new thing that was going to give him exactly what he needed. Then he would discuss with Rodney after the gym how much better he felt. And then he would discuss with Rodney on a soundstage after missing a few days of gym time how upset he was with himself, but that it was okay—he would be back on track soon. And then there would be the quiet non-discussion as he would send Rodney out to get him pizza and doughnuts.

Chris Campari was very into grooming products and waxing the surprising amount of ginger hair that grew on his back. Rodney was in charge of making sure that he got all the new and interesting things that he wanted. All the lotions and potions for his face. Rodney arranged the Botox injections that occasionally helped things out a little, and the outpatient thing for the tip of Chris's nose that he decided was drooping with age and needed to be turned back up. The discretion it took to step off the lot to have that little bit of surgery done and the terrible flu that had to be invented in order to buy and sell some recovery time.

And finally, there was Chris Campari's little son, who was entirely raised by a nanny and a preschool called "Kid Heaven." Rodney would occasionally have to go and check on the little boy or pick him up or drop him off or simply take some sort of person whom Chris Campari would occasionally hire for the preschoolers as a gift. A person with some kind of skill to impart for the day. A ventriloquist, a painting teacher, or, most recently, a life coach followed by an acting coach who showed the three-year-olds method acting techniques.

Rodney loved Chris for his enthusiasm. Even though Chris did almost all of the talking in their relationship, he did find it difficult to go on without Rodney. So this meant steady employment for Rodney, and in some ways, this gave Rodney a sense of purpose. It made him feel loved.

He felt that he had a reason to be there, skills that he was being paid for. He needed to feel the love of being needed. This at some point would foil him professionally, but at that moment it served him well. At the beginning of things, all the assistants really believed that they were special to Chris Campari. Later they would all find that he bonded briefly with anyone who was able to provide him with all his needs at any given moment. It was not personal. That is the greatest tragedy of the enabler, the false belief that they are indispensable.

So, after about an hour or so of spending time listening to this kind of talk about why Campari couldn't go to strip clubs anymore or why he could never do coke again because it made him so nuts and crazy and made him start thinking about his first girlfriend instead of loving his wonderful wife who stuck by him through thick and thin, Rodney would promise him that he wouldn't let him go to strip clubs anymore, just as he did every few months. At least one thing was for sure—if he did go to a strip club again, Rodney would certainly take away his cell phone because some of the late-night drink-and-dials would eventually get him into some sort of Internet or *Access Hollywood* trouble.

It was after one of these repentant talks that Rodney remembered that it was the day for the method acting teacher who'd been hired to go and teach the kids at Kid Heaven preschool.

Rodney was baffled as to how this would work out with the kids, being that the acting teacher was really for adults. But he gave up thinking it over once he realized he didn't even know what method acting was. All Rodney had to worry about was picking up the teacher and driving him to the school and waiting while the teacher gave his little class for the half hour, if the kids could focus their attention, and then taking the teacher back to where he got him from and coming back to the lot.

So he left and drove to Beverly Hills, where the pickup was, and was immediately struck by the acting teacher's appearance. He looked like someone who would be cast as a murderous villain in an action movie. Someone whose face was so far deep into adulthood that perhaps it had actually taken a turn towards a different species—as far as little kids were concerned. The extent of pockmarks and sagging flesh and fat in places children really hadn't thought about, and the splatter of dark moles that none of their daddies had or hair growing wildly from ears surely would alienate the kids right away. There was also the fact that the acting coach smelled quite heavily of cigarette smoke and that his voice was a strange sort of screech, possibly Eastern European in origin. And even if none of the aforementioned would upset the kids, surely the air of sternness he had about him would cement the whole thing together into something akin to childhood trauma.

But still, from what Rodney knew, there was never any telling. In his experience, things he thought could only go one way always surprised him by being able to go in ways he never thought of.

So they arrived at the preschool, found parking, and Rodney walked the method teacher in. The preschool was a transformed house in a residential neighborhood. The houses on either side had been bought up, and it had all been turned into a gated compound with outdoor play spaces and indoor playrooms cluttered with kids in different groups with names like the "Angels" or the "Cherubs," all separated by about a year or so. And then at age five, they would all be ejected into the world or wherever they went for real school.

Rodney always thought that this little preschool was actually more for the parents. Like a dog park where the owners come to meet each other, with their dogs as their excuse. The parents consisted of the rich and famous or just incredibly exotic mixtures of nationalities and races, the sort who would make a party seem very special. The parents liked to socialize with one another, but for the most part, as far as the kids were concerned, the things that happened in the preschool were the kinds of things they would neither remember nor, in Rodney's opinion, get any sort of edge in the world from. It was just an awful lot of money spent so the parents could have things to look forward to and perhaps feel less guilty about having their nannies and assistants bringing up their children.

So Rodney walked into the "Saints" class of three-year-olds, sat down, and waited for the method acting class. The monstrous-looking visiting teacher appeared from the bathroom, and Rodney could see immediately that some of the little kids were already beginning to get upset for reasons that they couldn't even understand.

The acting teacher began to speak. He gave a fairly brief account of what he taught, and then he asked the kids to raise their hands if they had questions.

Somehow the kids got the whole idea all wrong, thinking that it was something to do with growing lettuce and whatever else it was the three-year-olds came up with when they were only able to piece together bits of information without any real supervision. It was by far the most entertaining part of the whole thing for Rodney—hearing what strange assumptions they had come up with.

After a confusing and messy round of acting attempts and crying fits—being that preschoolers hate critique—the whole thing dissolved into tears and running around.

The acting coach rightly saw that it was time to end it.

"All right, kids, thank you for playing, and please help me thank young Mr. Campari for asking his dad for a class visitor."

The coach clearly didn't know the child's name, but once the kids heard his last name, they began chanting his first: "Angus, Angus, Angus!" The coach simply looked confused, and Rodney knew immediately that he had made a mistake by letting the chanting begin.

The five-year-old class was within earshot, and hearing the chanting, they began their own version of the chant: "Anus, Anus, Anus!" The three-year-olds didn't get it, and neither did Angus, but all the adults on the "Kid Heaven" compound cringed, yet were paralyzed about what do—since anything that was forbidden would simply become more alluring to the kids.

The chant sort of petered out, and the rest of the wrap-up went on without incident, with the coach not being quite as monstrous as Rodney had thought and the three-year-olds understanding nothing of the lesson in method acting. They were always being completely themselves. They had not grown self-conscious enough yet that they would need a class to teach them to be unselfconscious. They were pure, and their lives up to that point were one big theater of the unobserved.

But Rodney felt uneasy, as he always did when Angus's name came up around older kids. He wondered why on earth Chris had called his son that. After all, Chris was not Scottish. Surely he'd realized that what he'd done was hand his son a burden to carry. By age five, when his classmates would make the association that Angus sounded like a new word for butthole, it would all go downhill.

But until then, little Angus had a few years left in his own method world, before becoming self-conscious because of his name being so similar to the part of the anatomy that children love to talk about.

And by then Rodney thought perhaps he could spend a little special time with Angus and teach him how to punch and fight dirty. He was a small kid and a little bit overwhelmed by his father's huge personality and his mother's masculinity. The boy seemed in danger of falling into the gap between charisma and neglect.

But Rodney was alert. Rodney was there, waiting to save him.

*

The gym on the studio lot was basically in the

basement of one of the soundstages, which they had converted into a makeshift weight room and cardio space. The doctor had told Rodney that he needed to lose some weight, that his cholesterol was way too high, and that anything that was out of order in that way with his health would put too much pressure on his one lung, so he started to take his lunch and come down to the weight room and run on the treadmill.

There was hardly ever anyone else there, but once in a while he'd see some girls from other shows. Girls from wardrobe departments coming out to lose some weight. There was this one girl, funny-looking but cute too—she wasn't chubby or anything, she was real skinny, as a matter of fact—who'd come in and run.

Rodney would always smile at her but had no intention or anything towards her. She certainly wasn't his type. She had that whiteness where you almost imagine you could see her veins like on a shrimp or like a fetus, but he was friendly and wanted to make friends—especially with somebody he saw every day running and sweating up a storm.

But the girl wasn't all that friendly. He recognized her as being one of the wardrobe people from the soundstage next to his. She wore real fancy sweats with a matching top, and she frowned. Her lips would purse up over her slightly bucked front teeth, and her jaw would be so clenched up that her chin would get tiny little dimpling marks all over the front of it. It wasn't really a chin—it was more like where her mouth ended and her neck started—but still, there was something really attractive about her. She had a certain confidence, and even though her nose was big, it was not a distracting big. She seemed classy like there was something about her—like she had money—and he found himself really wanting her to give him her approval.

He didn't want to even really talk to her. He just wanted her to nod at him like in his old neighborhood. A weird little nodding acquaintance that would make them feel just a bit more cool. But she wouldn't look at him, and he didn't hold it against her. She probably was scared of getting hit on, and that must be a real pain in the ass—people constantly bothering you like that—so he let the whole thing go.

Then one day when he was loading up one of the trucks to do some returns and unloading some of the things out of the truck to be taken up to the production office, he saw a wardrobe trailer outside the stage where the skinny girl with the funny chin worked. She was handing out clothes from the back of the truck to all the extras, the actors who silently populated the backgrounds in shows.

He saw the skinny girl start talking to this one kid who was funny-looking—maybe a little slow—and the kid had a bunch of what looked like cranberry juice or wine or something all over the front of his shirt, and he saw the girl see the stain and start yelling at the kid.

Yelling: "What the hell is wrong with you? How could you have done that? Tell me exactly how it happened!"

And the kid just started stuttering, unable to answer, and saying "Sorry," and tears running down his face. The girl didn't even soften when she saw the tears. She just kept hollering, and she just kept saying, "Dude, what is wrong with you? Do you realize I have to clean that? Do you think of anyone but yourself? Maybe you shouldn't be drinking so much cranberry juice. Why did you even come here?"

Rodney felt something inside himself that he didn't like to feel. It was rage. A fury that only came along when he saw children and old people get harassed. This was the same feeling. Seeing somebody helpless with nobody to stick up for him getting pushed around by some lady for something really petty that he didn't even do on purpose.

He knew that, no matter what the extras did to their costumes, it was a production expense, and it was her job to clean the stain—or, rather, send it off to have cleaned. That's what she was getting union wages for.

Rodney knew that the kid hadn't done anything wrong except to show up to make crap money to get yelled at by people and eat cheap craft service just for a few bucks because he couldn't do any other work. He knew the fact that he even came out to do any kind of work was amazing when he could sit at home and watch TV all day and get fat and collect Social Security.

And here he was busting his butt. It had probably been fully explained to him that he'd never be a movie star and that he was never even going to meet any movie stars, because they'd never let him near any movie stars. But he came out and decided to work. He came out and decided to meet other people and to explore the world.

This was a brave young kid—and here he was getting dressed down by the chinless woman who probably did not have one single callous on either of her hands, let alone a bloody hole.

Rodney was muttering all of this under his breath. Just muttering and watching. He wished he could go back and somehow find some other way of saying "bloody hole," but he took a moment to breathe and went back to his righteous anger.

Soon Rodney started to realize that he'd gone too far in letting himself be upset—that he could feel his blood pressure rising. He could feel his stomach knotting up. His hands were getting sopping wet and hot. It seemed like, whenever he'd get his blood up, the stupid stigmata would really start to gush.

So he took another, deeper breath and thought, "Dear God, dear God, dear God. How could you let this happen to that kid? You see that woman? Punish her, God. Give her the weight of the world to carry. The weight of the world or the weight of a background artist's sadness or give her the weight of a black production assistant unloading Xerox paper while trying to not get blood on it. Putting paper onto a dolly so he can deliver it to people who don't understand that he's got one lung. I know my business isn't to show the people the error of their ways. If it's your will for me to watch and do nothing, I will. I know my will is not your will, but dear God, you put some weight on her shoulders so she can feel what it's like.... So she can walk a mile in those shoes and so she can really start to understand what it's like to be somebody other than herself."

It was as if God wanted him to see everything about this skinny wardrobe woman as being completely unjust.

At the end of the day, while he was coming back from his third or fourth run for supplies, stuck in traffic sweating, unloading more paper because the first batch had been the wrong kind, and he had to take it back, stuck in a traffic jam sweating with no A/C, and he had finally come back with the right paper and unloaded it all over again onto the dolly, he looked over and saw that the TV show the girl worked for was wrapping for the day.

Just as he looked up, he saw a brand spanking new shiny BMW drive by with the girl with no chin sitting in it, and she sneered at him. He saw her sneer at him, and he just took a deep breath again and said: "Dear God, is this some kind of joke? Are you kidding me? She's got a BMW, and she's a bad person, and she sneered at me? Come on now, come on, God, what are you doing? At least, God, grant me the serenity not take up the things I cannot change, the courage to change the things I can, and the wisdom to know the difference. And, Lord, I really do think she tried to run me down when she drove by. Just want to make sure you saw that."

He didn't see the girl again for a while and got preoccupied with his work, so he pushed her awfulness out of his mind. He still went to the gym, but his schedule changed up a bit. So he went at a different time than when he usually saw the girl, and he was glad of that.

He found that the more he worked out, the more he was getting into shape. His body started to really straighten out. The fat around his middle and even on his hips started to disappear—just melting off like mad—five pounds a week. He was looking good, feeling better, and running just a little bit, not even every day. Three days a week he'd climb down the stairs to that musty basement at the bottom of the soundstage, get on the treadmill, and look at himself in the mirror instead of looking over at the televisions.

He'd just look at himself and watch his steps— always running slowly so as not to hurt his lung. He was losing five pounds a week. Sometimes he thought he was losing seven.

He gave up weighing himself. It was just too exciting—he looked good, and the ladies were noticing. All the females were saying hello to him, and nice ones too. Some in golf carts would drive by him as he walked back all sweaty, back to work. They'd roll by and say "Hi there," while looking him up and down.

He felt like he wasn't so invisible anymore. He had been about 230 pounds, and in the last few weeks he'd lost at least forty, and he liked it. Now he wanted to lose ten more.

He had lost a bunch of weight one other time on Weight Watchers. He'd loved that Weight Watchers— the food, the meetings they had where all the ladies sat around with you and told you what kind of tricks you could use to lose weight and still eat what you wanted. That's where he learned all about frozen yogurt—the chocolate kind with the brownies that was like one-third as fatty as ice cream.

It seemed like the easiest thing in the world, counting points, and he did and lost something like fifty pounds, but he didn't know what happened. Somehow he got sick, his lung was giving him trouble, and it just seemed like way too much to think about counting points and eating right. He let the whole thing go, went into this big shame about it, and didn't want to try losing weight again. He pretended that the whole weight thing was an old issue that didn't even exist, until the doctor told him he had to lose it again.

He was still too ashamed to go back to Weight Watchers and tell the ladies how he had let them down and how he had strayed from the path. He decided to do the workout thing and just sort of try eating more carrots and fewer doughnuts, and there he was losing five, six, seven, eight pounds a week.

While he didn't know what was going on, he had a vague feeling it might be stigmata-related, because he was losing a lot of blood too. One lunchtime, after Rodney got back early from one of his errands, he decided to go to the gym at a different time than his most recent schedule had allowed. He saw the golf cart from the skinny girl's TV show parked outside the soundstage where the gym was. His heart lurched with recalled anger as he pictured her yelling at the slow kid. He didn't want to feel that anger again but wondered if that's the way the Lord wanted it. So he paused briefly to let the anger pass, then climbed down the stairs leading to the gym.

At this point, he had lost about fifty pounds. With every five pounds he'd lost, not only did he feel lighter in person, but in spirit too.

He stepped into the gym and looked around to see who was there, but there was just one heavyset lady on a treadmill. He thought, "If she only knew about counting points.... If she only knew when you've got chocolate brownie frozen yogurt waiting at home for you, you'd never eat a craft service doughnut again. If it wasn't so rude, I'd tell her about Weight Watchers. Tell her she has nice hair and nice eyes—why not take care of your..."

He stopped mid-thought. The woman he was looking at was the skinny girl from the show. She was no lady. She'd just packed on many, many pounds. Rodney was shocked and couldn't stop gaping. Like one of those naturally skinny people who'd never gained weight, she had gotten fat without seeing it coming.

The odds that she had gotten fat from fried food were low but possible. Had she just eaten too many grilled garden burgers?

But then she'd caught on and given up. She looked like she'd gone out there and set her mind to it and just started to eat all the things she used to avoid. So maybe fried food had come into play.

Somebody came out of the ladies' room, and he realized that the girl was not alone. He looked at them and tried not to look at them for too long, to not be rude. He heard them talking—the gym was otherwise empty, so their voices carried. Sometimes women talked around him like he was foreign, like he wouldn't even understand what they were saying. It was weird—it wasn't that they thought he was a dog or that he wasn't American and didn't speak English—but they just talked like he wasn't even there.

"I don't know what the fuck is going on with my body, and I went to the doctor and had my thyroid checked. I'm not sure what's happening. I started gaining at least five pounds a week, then it went up to seven, and now it's eight. I've gained fifty fucking pounds. No matter what I eat, no matter how much I work out…. And the doctor said there's nothing wrong with my thyroid, and they don't know what it is. They're acting like I'm eating secretly and not admitting it.... Like I have an eating disorder. They said, 'You know this can't be happening if you haven't been eating and there's nothing wrong with your thyroid.' I am going out of my fucking mind!"

She was practically crying on the workout machine. Rodney couldn't believe it and tried not to let her see him stare.

She did see him but didn't recognize him. She just felt a pang of grief for how attractive he was and how unavailable to her new fat self a guy like him would be.

Her colleague was intrigued and horrified by her crazy weight gain but said nothing and simply listened to her rant in astonishment.

"Maybe it's all my money issues—people's bodies give in to stress and deal differently, and you know, I don't know, maybe the therapist can come up with some explanation, and it might just be that we have the capacity to gain weight so we can coat ourselves with fat and feel protected and maybe we can do that without eating. Like a porcupine has needles or whatever the fuck.... Of course, if we could do it without eating, all those people starving in Africa and, you know, wherever else would probably be psychologically gaining weight as well. I'm not saying that it's literal, but I'm just saying maybe that's what's happening because I know I have said and I've sworn up and down I'm not getting up in the middle of the night and taking out the Chunky Monkey or anything. At least not at first. Maybe it's just something a therapist needs to take a look at and figure out."

She started to pray. This was what she'd been doing as a last resort—praying out loud and calling God's name right in public.

Her companion immediately jumped off the treadmill and said, "I'll see you on set," and practically ran out of the gym. People will tolerate a lot, but talking out loud to God is the limit for most.

Rodney felt himself puff up a little when he heard the woman mentioning God. He was startled and happy but annoyed, too—he didn't want God on her side.

Sometimes he didn't think anyone understood God the way they should, and it made him feel indignant and protective of God. People just talked about him like he was some kind of favor-giver or a punisher. God was bigger than that. Rodney knew that not everybody felt gratitude and was filled with the Holy Spirit the way he'd been taught to try and be.

At his church, there was singing and rejoicing, because there was a belief that God could hear them, and an open channel of communication existed. So when he heard that funny girl in the gym talking about and to God, he remembered something that made his thoughts come to a screeching halt. He remembered that one of the last pleading conversations he had had with God had been about this woman.

Well, of course, he did have conversations with God every day, begging him to stop the stigmata and the bleeding from his hands, but the last conversation he had that involved another person was about this woman. He had asked God to put the weight of the world on her shoulders.

He realized that his feet had stopped moving and that he'd glided to the back of the treadmill as if on one of those walkways at the airport that takes you from the terminal to the exit because it's so damn far and everybody is lazy. He had just come to the end of the treadmill, and it had stopped from the lack of motion from his feet.

He felt a chill all over. He'd started to sweat, and the sweat made him cold.

Rodney was making the girl in the gym fat. Or, he believed, God was taking the weight he was losing so quickly and putting it on her.

This thought freaked Rodney out completely, and he had to hop off the treadmill, on which he'd been standing quite still for some time, and run to the exit.

He could tell that the woman saw him but didn't recognize him as being the guy she would occasionally see loading and unloading stuff right near her wardrobe truck. She even looked at him with longing.

Rodney went upstairs for air. He stood outside and slowly calmed down while considering the facts.

He was bleeding from his hands all day, every day, and he hadn't died yet, so who knows what else was possible. What was impossible in his mind wasn't relevant anymore; it was more the question of why. Why did God want him to bleed from his hands? Why would God want him to lose weight so easily and survive with one lung, and to put weight on a bad woman?

What was the purpose, and what was the big picture? And what was expected of him in return for these gifts, if they were actually gifts?

Rodney had no idea, and he asked every night in his prayers to be shown.

*

He had been born in the summer of 1964, so Rodney was not a young man anymore. In the summer of 1964, he was a brand-new baby—a brand-new white baby, according to his grandmother, but by 1967 he was a black child.

He had gone overnight from being a small white baby to being a regular black toddler, and this had been a shock to his white mother and caused problems in her neighborhood, and so she had found a black family and had given Rodney over to them because her husband was not black, nor even alive.

Only his grandmother told this story, and considering that she was an honest and God-fearing woman, it seemed odd for her to tell such a bald-faced lie.

His dad, Rodney Senior, was not only perfectly black, but he looked quite a bit like Rodney, Jr. There was a powerful family resemblance that adoption would not have allowed. There were also inherited interests passed down from Senior to Junior. Rodney's dad had worked in the theater and later on soundstages and on film sets, just as he himself did now. He had been handed the job by his cousin, John, rather than following the passion his father had had. But, still, it seemed like more evidence that he was in the family by blood. Blood, blood, blood.

But there were other stories that he knew to be true and also related to a white mother. Rodney remembered bits of it vaguely from when he was a child. It went like this: his father had for a time left the family because he had met a white woman at the theater and took up with her while her husband was away at war. But then something had happened, and this is where the story got vague—his father had come right back, and his mother had forgiven him, and they never talked about it anymore.

He remembered one great big fight where his mother had taken a box out into the yard and had ripped and torn up a bunch of things from the box that seemed to be papers. And Rodney had moved toward the papers and realized that they were actually letters and looked like lady letters on paper the color of marshmallows—pale yellow like baby clothes, the way female things are. His mother had torn and ripped those pieces of paper up really well, and then she threw them into the firepit in the back of the yard. And Rodney remembered thinking that it probably had something to do with the lady his dad had run off with all of those years before, and that maybe he'd saved some souvenirs and his mother found them.

That was exactly what had happened.

When Rodney had gotten sick, and it turned out that something was wrong with his lung, his cousin had come to the rescue and really been there for him. He lost the lung, but mostly he got a stronger sense of gratitude for his family.

Rodney had promised his family that he would really clean up and take one of the jobs that his cousin got him at the soundstage.

A job that his own mother never approved of because it reminded her too much of his own dad working at the theater way back when—the Alex Theatre in Glendale. But a job was a job.

Still, it was the first time Rodney really thought about life and what he could do with it. Not just pass time from one thing to the next or wait for something to happen but really do something every day.

Rodney was no longer ever short of money, and he got to help his mother and help the family, and so the only thing left was to find love and maybe start a family and become a dad himself.

But the bleeding hands had started, and then he had put on some weight from eating from the anxiety of everything and not really getting used to the new diet of less salt, less fat, and all that stuff. He had to take off some of that weight, and then he started to fixate on the bad woman at work, and all kinds of things were distracting him. All that traffic couldn't have been good for his health.

Rodney just didn't feel right, even after getting fit. How could he ask anyone on a date with bleeding hands?

But still, he knew he had to be grateful anyway. Every night he would pray for his dearly departed father and his alive and in-charge mother and cousin. Then he thanked God for his job. And then he thanked God for his health and asked God for help in understanding the things going on around him that he simply didn't know what to make of—like the bleeding.

Rodney knew there was somebody else in charge of his life. It was a good feeling, and it was good to know that he didn't have to make anything happen anymore. All he had to do was let things happen, and all he had to do was get up, suit up, and show up. Wait to see what would happen next. It was a strange feeling, and the closest thing to being a child again, except it felt like this big new parent that he now had was magical and strange, in that any number of players in any number of situations could be put into motion by his power.

It was really like watching a movie except that it was his own life, and he was a player with all kinds of other people involved who were very real. Sometimes it scared him when he lay awake at night and thought about it like that—but still, he liked it.

People had always told Rodney that he was a great listener. In school, all the girls would come to him to tell him all their secrets, tell him what boys they liked, and at the end of talking to him they always would finish it off with, "Rodney, you are such a good listener. You are such a good friend."

Rodney thought about how the girls didn't really want to go with the good listener. They wanted to go with the bad boy who would ignore them, then they could tell all their woes to the good listener. Someone had told him that the right girl would actually understand that the good listener was the one to be with. Still, Rodney knew that he wasn't a good listener so much because he was interested in the person or what it was that they were saying, but more that he was listening to hear a clue—to gather clues so he could understand what it all meant. "It" being life.

He wanted to know if there was some answer that would make everything make sense to him. He wanted so much to understand, that everywhere he went he listened intently. He found life in the world so baffling sometimes and his role in it so incomprehensible, as if he had been told to show up to a place to do a job, but that no one was there to tell him what that job was—all he could do was listen carefully to any person who spoke to him, hoping somehow to find out what his own calling was through the information he could glean from them and their lives.

It took Rodney a long time to understand this about himself. For a long time, he had simply thought maybe he was a good person or maybe he was a caring person, and although he did care, he mostly listened to find himself.

He would smile and nod every time somebody would begin to speak, and something about the action of his smiling and nodding would make them speak more and more and more, and somehow there would be a bond, but the bond would be from only one side.

The person speaking would feel a tremendous bond to Rodney, and Rodney, ultimately, by the end of it, would feel somewhat embarrassed and a little more lost than before—strange and lonely.

He noticed that the people who needed to be listened to the most also asked the fewest questions. They were the ones who wanted to know the least about him, but they had a lot to say. It was a strange paradox that the person who wanted to be heard the most could not hear himself.

Rodney tried not to judge, and perhaps that was another key to why people told him things. They could feel his non-judgment, but again they thought it was because he was kind and good. He found that if he was judgmental, it was more difficult for him to hear the messages and understand what his role was. But if he was able to just listen impartially, he could find all kinds of hints in all kinds of people.

For instance, at the hospital Rodney had met an old Persian man and had begun to talk to him and continued to go back and visit him once he, himself, had been discharged. He had learned so much from this unlikely man even though he found him to be childish, self-absorbed, and not a good man at all. He'd left wives and kids behind, and he talked a lot about himself and how he was better than everyone, which made him seem ridiculous. There wasn't anything about him in any way attractive to Rodney other than the fact that he could tell he made the man happy by listening to him.

And while he made him happy by listening, Rodney himself learned tons of stuff from him. Things about why we were here and about why youth was so important and why therefore it had to pass so quickly.

The man had told him that when you're young you are a god, and if we all stayed young we would all be gods. It was important for us to be godly for a brief time and not know it and then have it taken from us so that we could write about it and muse on it and feel encouraged to give birth so that we could see that godliness in our youngsters.

And somehow the whole thing was designed by

a bigger God so that if we were to stay young men, there would be no bigger God and we would take over, and that would not be good.

This was so astonishing and lovely to Rodney that he wanted to talk about this again with the old man. But the old man could not remember telling him that or had somehow changed his mind. He instead said that there was no God and the youth are idiots.

He found that sometimes the old man gave kernels of wisdom despite himself, despite his own smallness of spirit and narrow range of personality. Sometimes when he was on Demerol or sometimes when he was especially frightened of death, he told the truth, but once he felt better, once he was off the medications and was back on Earth, he took back all the wisdom he had given out.

But mostly, Rodney liked when the Persian man's daughter visited him. They would draw the curtain so Rodney could only hear their voices—like a story. He would listen to the young woman ask her father question after question about their lives and his reasons for everything. And she would laugh while he answered, or get upset, or simply sigh. Either way, the love they passed between them seemed to have survived all his selfishness and her disappointment.

It reminded Rodney of those jobs that were so fancy that they had "closing interviews," where they talked to you about how working there had been, as they were firing you or you were quitting on them. The old man's daughter was giving him his closing interview, and it seemed that, despite everything, she would be recommending him to his next post.

At work, Rodney found that all the departments had liked him coming up to say hello. They'd all perk up and say, "Rodney, Rodney, how you been?" People just saw him and liked him, and that's why his cousin had gotten him the job. Rodney was gentle but knew karate. His attention and interest made people feel good. He was like the kind of dog that everyone wanted to pet because, even though he could kill you, he never would. He was like the baby that made everyone feel like taking care of him.

And because he inspired trust and love, people would start telling him things, like my wife is not my greatest love, and the kids leave me cold, and money's too tight to mention. And Rodney would reply, "Yeah, I hear you. Well.... Everything will be okay."

Sometimes Rodney thought that it was all the listening that he was doing and all the focus on the other person that made it possible for him to walk around with two bleeding hands for all those months and have nobody even notice yet. People rarely looked at any part of him when they saw him—maybe his eyes and teeth for a minute. But mostly, when they spoke to Rodney, people just looked inward.

Chapter Four

The Sponsor

THE SPONSOR WAS SITTING in a lotus position and doing her best to ignore her own rapid ruminations. She tried to filter or empty her mind of all thought.

She sat at the Buddhist center where she had been spending more and more of her time—something that her husband did not seem to mind, which disappointed her somewhat. She knew that did not mean he didn't love her, and he certainly showed his love. But she needed huge demonstrations of the stuff, and her husband's love sometimes felt a bit sparse.

She sat in the lotus position, smelled the incense, and listened to the tinkling wind chimes that hung in the windows. In the distance, she heard the whispering of the young people, with their tattoos and dyed hair. All of them looking for salvation, or at least serenity, after having not found it in ink parlors and twelve-step meetings.

She began to hear their conversations and once again tried to empty her mind for what seemed to be the tenth time.

She suddenly felt someone put down their mat and sit next to her. The person had oddly chosen to sit so close, even though the large room was unoccupied. This, of course, irritated her, and she had to bring her mind back down to a calm and peaceful place and to tell herself that everything happened for a reason. She didn't want to peek, but she did. She opened her eyes because she needed to see who it was that she was feeling and fighting back her annoyance about.

And who was next to her but the famous actor, Chris Campari, from the show *Wolf Brigade*. And sure enough, he was looking right back at her, smiling sheepishly.

"Hi, my name's Chris."

"Hello, I'm Mary."

"I know it's cheesy to be doing this, but you know I wanted to give it a shot."

He smiled a huge smile after saying this, and she was done for— hook, line, and sinker. She proceeded to reassure him how it was actually fantastic that he was there and that he was looking for something beyond his daily superficial life, et cetera, et cetera.

He nodded and seemed to drink it all in with his blue eyes, which poured back a light onto her in a way that no one had in years. And she felt that, yes, indeed, there has been a reason for everything, and here was a man who needed her—a young man who was going to listen to her advice.

And so she proceeded to advise him about how

to meditate and how to grapple with Buddhism and with the material world and so on and so forth.

He listened and nodded humbly. He kept saying, "I can't tell you how much I appreciate this," and "Thank you so much."

They kept talking, and soon he was telling her about his upbringing and how he had grown up partly in Canada, partly in Los Angeles, partly in Texas, and partly in New York, shuffled around among grandparents. He told her the hilarious story of having been caught masturbating in the bathroom by his grandmother, slathering conditioner onto his erection and using a ruler to measure how long it was. The sponsor never once considered the appropriateness of such divulgences but felt special and sexy that he would share such stories with her.

They laughed about his penis quietly, and the sponsor felt infinitely lucky for her sudden intimacy with the famous actor.

She told him that she was thinking about becoming more involved with the meditation center and maybe taking whatever classes she needed to take to become an instructor or healer or whatever. They had recently asked her to join their board of directors, and despite the initial fee they wanted for her joining, she knew it was her advice they really sought.

Chris Campari seemed fascinated and impressed with her story. She loved how he showed that he was impressed and didn't hide it, and how he gushed. He gently touched her knee as she was sitting in the lotus position, over and over again. He finally said the very thing that the sponsor lady didn't know she needed to hear in order to feel like a human being:

"Maybe you can have a meditation thing, you know, at my ranch. I'm sure my wife wouldn't mind. We can certainly learn from you, and you could come over and invite some of your people and, you know, just take over. Maybe we'll have some writers come and see how you are leading the meditation. Am I being stupid?" He started laughing and even pretended so well to be embarrassed that he drew blood to his face.

He was basically saying everything the sponsor wished every man she ever met who was young and confused, who reminded her of her own youth and made her feel pretty, would say. He was basically saying what she wished they could all at least be thinking. He called her "his possible guru," and she felt like she was going to start crying. Like she wanted him to love her even more, and she wanted to show him her love by opening him up and crawling inside him. Her sense of self suddenly became solid because someone was propping it up, and she thought that now she could do anything.

As they were speaking, the light was changing, and it seemed as if they'd been there for hours. She heard someone whisper across the room at them, and Chris Campari turned and saw that it was somebody he knew. He gasped and said, "Oh, my God, I can't believe it," and jumped up and said excuse me to the sponsor and walked over to the friend standing at the entrance.

The sponsor waited for them to say hello and for him to get back to his conversation with her. But he didn't. He continued to talk and talk with his friend for what seemed like at least half an hour.

The sponsor slowly turned back to her meditation position and began to try to go back to what she was doing. But she couldn't stop thinking about Chris Campari, and she couldn't stop having a vague resentment that he'd walked away and hadn't come back to their conversation. But she took solace that his little mat and sweater were sitting right next to her, and that he would be back.

She turned around and saw that he wasn't there, but she could see him through the open door in the parking lot having a cigarette with his friend, and then they were joined by a woman whom Chris Campari touched on the shoulder when addressing. They started talking more seriously, and the dusk grew darker.

The sponsor glanced over at his sweater and mat and thought, "He'll be right back."

She exercised enormous concentration and turned her mind from worrying about someone else's behavior. She told herself that she had made an incredible connection with this man and that they were about to embark on the next phase of a friendship. So she meditated probably with more concentration and steadiness than she had ever had. She let herself accept something good that may have happened to her and let herself be in it.

Finally, after what seemed like perhaps another hour, she heard a rustling next to her and opened her eyes and turned. It was Chris Campari picking up his sweater and slowly walking away.

He saw her see him, and he took on the abashed face of a naughty boy.

"I'm so sorry, but I didn't want to interrupt your meditation, so I was tiptoeing. I just saw some really old friends, and we're gonna go catch up some more. It was really great talking to you."

He squeezed her shoulder, and she was sure the next thing he was going to say was "Let's exchange information," or "I'll see you here tomorrow," or something like that. She was stunned when he didn't and found herself unable to speak, to maybe initiate this herself. Instead, she let him walk out.

He turned one more time and waved and gave an almost apologetic shrug of the shoulders as he ran out to join the people waiting for him, jumping up and down increasingly fast when he got to them. They ran to their cars and headed to whatever fancy restaurant they were going to.

The sponsor turned back around, her face and eyes burning with tears as she heard from across the room someone say: "You've been meditating for two whole hours, that is amazing. How are you? Must be feeling so good."

"Have I?" she replied. "I'd better get going."

She got up, picked up her mat and sweatshirt, and headed out towards the parking lot. She felt an incredible sense of shame and stupidity. She began to berate herself in her head in a way that she had not in some time.

"Stupid old cow! How could you even be so fucking delusional to think that you are about to be best pals with a movie star? He just led you on.... And it was so easy. And suddenly you felt like you weren't a loser? Like he'd take you away from your miserable self? Like he'd give you a little bit of that fucking fame. You could get some crumbs off his table? But you're not even good enough for that, you've never done anything with yourself, you're just a hanger-on and a groupie."

She cried quietly, and perhaps if the self-reproach were not so mean she could have used its underlying truths to empower herself. If the internal voices did not loathe her so, she might have heard their message of self-reliance and creative self-fulfillment. But they were too harsh, so their message was lost. The pain her berating voices caused the sponsor was too great, and she dismissed her inner voice as an enemy and a liar in order to keep on living.

*

Even though she was fifty-eight years old, she didn't really understand it. As time went on, she didn't see herself as others did, and in some ways, the yearning that she had at age twenty and age thirty and even age forty or so was much the same.

She did not realize that perhaps she should have developed a new set of desires that would suit her better. It was only when she spent time with her sponsees that she realized how much time had passed. It wasn't that she noticed how young they were; it was the reverence with which they treated her—the reverence that a younger woman has for an older one. And this, instead of making her feel good, somehow put her ill at ease.

She was driving along on a particular afternoon feeling somewhat maligned, frightened, and caught out in a way, because she'd been called out about a certain behavior of hers by one of her young sponsees. One of the newer ones who she hadn't thought would call her out on something like that, considering that the girl seemed a little bit enamored of her. The young sponsee had pretty much called it like she saw it, and the sponsor was left in the lurch trying to come up with some excuse for what she had done and had been caught doing.

She'd been counseling the girl for a few months, and a lot of the problems the girl was having weren't about alcohol anymore but about underlying feelings, and a lot of those were anger and confusion directed at her boyfriend. She would confide in the sponsor about the feelings, and the sponsor would grow increasingly anxious, since she did know the girl's boyfriend from meetings and had found herself growing fond of him. And in some older-sister way (although the boyfriend would have said "motherly way" because of the age difference that he could see but the sponsor could not), she had insinuated herself into his life—checking up on him or on his children, making sure to remember his birthday, and sending cards. Even though the sponsor was married—and, she felt, happily married—she had a few younger men such as the sponsee's boyfriend whom she liked to make herself somehow useful to. She enjoyed the energy she exchanged with them—not something she would call flirtatious but rather, lively.

So the sponsor drove, thinking about how suddenly the nice admiring face the sponsee had been wearing for the past few months had dropped, and the anger that she had up until that point expressed towards other people—mainly her boyfriend—had suddenly turned on her. And when it turned, it turned hard. The girl had raised her voice and said:

"I've put up with your shit when you called me a hater and a rager—neither word being in the vocabulary that's used in the program nor anything that has anything to do with the twelve steps. Words you used out of frustration and stupidity. You blurted them out at me, judging me and putting me down and raising your sad self up. I've let those things go, and I've enjoyed some of your better bits of advice, but now you've gone too far."

Then she said, "What I want to ask you is, what exactly is your agenda? What is it that you're after? And can you even figure out how inappropriate what you did is? I don't know what to tell you beyond that.... All I know is that you need to get the fuck away from me, my boyfriend, my home, my family, and everything that I care about, because you're creepy."

The sponsor had played and replayed the whole thing in her head. She was just grateful that it had happened over the phone and not in person. She could imagine the young sponsee's fiery poker face. The girl's articulateness with words and emotions made her a strange and striking person—one the sponsor had hoped to break down to a normal sort of thing, or at least to an average femaleness rather than the heightened hyper-natural beauty with an edge of the dangerous drunk that the girl had been, up to that point.

But the reality was that the drunk part was long gone, and what remained was the rest of the girl's personality. It would not be normalized or tamed so as not to threaten the sponsor. The girl was incredibly sharp, and the sponsor was regretting very much, at that moment, having put herself on the receiving end of the girl's disapproval.

What the sponsor had done, basically, was in a

way semi-unconscious. As a suggestion to heighten the bond and get closer to her boyfriend, the sponsor lady had suggested that the girl take on projects she needed to do and that she bookend these things to avoid procrastination. And she suggested that she bookend these things with her boyfriend—bookending meaning giving a call or touching base with somebody before you begin the task, and when you're done with the task touching base again, telling them you've completed it or calling them or maybe talking to them halfway through the task, punctuating incrementally the time and effort it takes to do such a thing. These bookending actions prevent lazy people from just letting the whole thing go and not doing it at all. The sponsor had suggested to the girl that it was an intimate and interesting project to take on with her boyfriend. They could get closer and overcome things like their procrastination: a trust exercise that could enmesh their lives a little bit.

This was the most practical and interesting bit of advice the sponsor had given her sponsee, and she quickly jumped at it and was very grateful. She went home, but just as she was about to start telling her boyfriend, something came up, and she forgot all about it. A few days passed, and she was just about to tell him again about the whole thing when the phone rang. Her boyfriend went to answer it, and she heard him talking on the phone for a while, and when he got off, he said, "Hey, that was Mary."

The sponsee asked what the woman had called about—after all, she did call the boyfriend occasionally since they were pals, and he replied:

"Oh, well, actually she wanted to do some bookending with me since she's been procrastinating on some things, and she thought it would be a good idea for her and me to do some work together. What do you think? Seems like a good way for me to get some stuff done, huh?"

And so that's how it started. The girl told her boyfriend about the suggestion that the woman had made to her, that it would be a good closeness/enmeshment thing to do with the boyfriend, and then had herself swooped in for said enmeshment.

Then the girl got on the phone and pretty much tore the sponsor a new asshole. So, in turn, the sponsor had to call her own sponsor, and they had to talk about agendas and motives, and she had to look at why she did it. Even though she told her sponsor that she just hadn't been thinking, she knew perfectly well what she had been thinking. In some strange way, she was being envious, and she was moving in on the girl's boyfriend and basically competing with a woman who was young enough to be her daughter. It was a strange move and a grotesque move, especially grotesque because of her time in the world of the sane and sober.

But the sponsor's own sponsor, who was also somewhat crazy and regularly did things that were highly inappropriate herself, told the sponsor that she hadn't really done anything wrong. After all, she'd known the boyfriend for some time, and whoever heard of not bookending with more than one person?

So the sponsor felt a little bit let off the hook by her own sponsor, but she knew deep down where her conscience lay—the small voice of her moral compass. It was always there, even though she tried to bury it with lists of things she wanted to do with her life. The voice told her the ugly truth every time. She knew what she had done, and she knew it was wrong.

She pulled into a parking structure, on her way to meet her husband for lunch, and she was simply out of her mind by then. The sponsor imagined what the girl would tell everyone—because of the power of what she had said to her. The sponsor shuddered, knowing full well that the girl wasn't going to keep this private or a secret. Not only was she sure to tell her boyfriend, but she'd be sure to tell every person she knew in AA. And if she saw her again, she was probably going to tell the sponsor off again too.

And then she felt a rage at the girl. How dare she?

The sponsor talked out loud to herself: "I can do whatever I want! I've known him for a long time! I can bookend with whomever I want, and it's none of her business. Who is she to tell me who to be friends with? I am her sponsor; she doesn't tell me what to do."

But the sponsor knew her rant wouldn't hold up to scrutiny. The sponsee could come up to her and spit in her face and get up in front of the whole room—a hundred people—and tell them that she was a dirty old lady who had crossed the sacred line of sponsor/sponsee trust and had tried to move in on her boyfriend because she was a lonely wretch. Somehow being called lonely was the worst insult she could think of. And there wouldn't be one person in the room who would not think: "Yeah lady, what are you doing calling your sponsee's boyfriend?"

The sponsor pulled into a parking space after spiraling upwards towards the roof of the packed structure for some time. The lights were dim, and she turned and accelerated too quickly to stop when she realized there was already a car in the space. It had been pulled in so far that it was not visible until she was right behind it and crunching its rear with her front bumper. It was a brand-new BMW, and it mangled up like aluminum foil. The sponsor pulled back and just stared at the ruined rear of the shiny new car. The damage looked like marks in fresh cement or a flaw in cake icing. Her eye desperately wanted to fix it. And, as if that were not bad enough, the trunk of the car flew open.

She herself had just bought a new used car. Something, she'd been told by her therapist, she had not loved herself enough to get until then. She'd been driving the same old piece-of-crap Nissan for years and years, the paint peeling off it like a bad sunburn. Now, finally, she had something of a decent car, and here she was ramming into a really decent car—a new car with expensive parts and probably an owner with great coverage who would suck the repair money out of the sponsor and destroy her since she hadn't renewed her insurance yet.

She sat there and looked around and immediately went back into the sort of thinking that a drunk thinks. She looked around to see if anyone saw what she did. She looked around to see if there were any cameras. And having seen neither witnesses nor surveillance, she pulled back, turned around, and drove right out of the parking structure and off the movie lot she had driven to for lunch. She was calm while calling her husband on her cell phone to say she was feeling sick and couldn't make it for lunch.

She drove away as fast as she could from what she had done, and she cried and laughed and didn't know what to do anymore. She felt like she didn't have twenty years of sobriety at all. She felt like a dumb junkie chick from the Valley, just like she'd always been, and that's how it went as she drove herself home.

The sponsor let herself into the house, petted the cats, lay down on the sofa, and cried like a child.

Back in the parking structure, a cool concrete breeze rustled the letters that sat exposed in the trunk of the crunched BMW. The impact of the crash had knocked the lid off the shoebox that held the letters. The pages sent their messages out into the wind.

*

He had drunk on the new liver, and that was the shame of it. He had been waiting on a list to get a fresh new young liver after ravaging the one he had been born with, with alcohol and drugs for years and years, and once he had received the fresh new liver of a youth wasted in a car accident, and after vowing to enjoy his second chance and be grateful and humbly taking it and swearing off all things bad and self-destructive, after taking the thing into his body and popping all the pills, all the expensive anti-rejection pills, what he had done was to go back to drinking and to drink so heavily as to actually rot away the new liver too.

And that was the shame of it. That is what burned the sponsor and got to her the most—the fact that he was so unsympathetic that she could not even love her brother after death without a pang of guilt that the man she had loved and now mourned—the little boy whose diapers she had changed—was an unstoppable adult lunatic with no sense of decency.

She wanted to be angry. She wanted to go along with the rest of the family and spit on his grave and say: "You know what? You brought this on yourself! Go to hell! Go to hell!"

He took that liver from somebody. He took it from somebody who could have lived on, but instead he fought and pleaded and got himself on all kinds of lists and took life from someone else, and then he drank all night, every night, and he died.

He drank on the fresh pain, the liver of a teenage

kid who died before his time, and he drank on the liver that could've belonged to another teenage kid who was dying, in order to live and drink some more.

What he did was sit around in his own shit in his dark house with all the utilities shut off. He wouldn't get up to pay his bills, so he drank in the dark. And he died in the dark, and he smelled up the place. Then they had to clean up after him, and then they were supposed to mourn him as well.

But the sponsor couldn't take that attitude, and she couldn't take their rage. All she could think about was her tiny little brother in diapers, how some sort of monster had taken him and held him for most of his life, and that they'd not been able to get the monster to leave. That some parasite had lived in him and made him do those things just as it had in her. Just as it had ravaged her, but she got away. She got sober, but the little baby brother in the diapers didn't.

He never got his life back, and the parasite lived on. Nobody seemed to remember that there was a difference between the sweet young brother and the animal that lived inside him.

She felt ashamed for feeling that way, but she did, and she wanted to somehow go back in time and save him or go forward in time and save people like him. All she knew was that it made her sick to her stomach whenever she thought about it, and she wanted to walk around in circles in her house and bang her head on the walls and tear out chunks of her hair.

She just couldn't believe that it was allowed to happen—that he was allowed to die.

It was also hard to be grateful for what she had. The thing that drove her crazy about some people's lives, especially people like the sponsee, was just the fact that everything came so easily to them.

That these lovely, wonderful, loyal men would throw themselves at their feet, that fantastic jobs came their way, that life just sort of blossomed at their touch, and yet they were full of complaints and piss and vinegar, and when she would say "You should be happy that he doesn't lie to you or cheat on you, be happy that you're making twenty-seven bucks an hour, or aren't you just happy to be alive?"—they would look at her like she was a desperate old lady who hadn't had a whole lot in her life, so her bottom line was very low, and so what she was ready to be excited about was so very little compared to what it was they felt they deserved.

The worst part was that it was true.

The sponsor thought about making dinner and then remembered quickly that she didn't like to make dinner and was a terrible cook. Her husband would be home soon and would take care of it, so she sat down on her meditation mat and decided to do a little meditating.

She had become involved with a young man and his Buddhism group. They sold T-shirts and had books and all kinds of urban, modern, accessible, liberal ways about explaining this old Buddhism thing to everyone, and it was charming and fascinating. This young man gave her the sort of attention that made her feel alive and useful. He had asked her to be on the board of directors, and she had felt special and important. She had said she would think about it, and then she decided even before she began to think about it that when the time came, and he asked her again, she would indeed say yes. And so she was grateful and sat on the mat and decided to focus just on that joy.

But that's not how it went. The voices clamored, and her head was a cacophony that she only heard when she was attempting to be quiet. It was one loud, obnoxious accusation after the next:

"You are pretending to be a Buddhist. You know that girl is right about you, and you're nothing but a fraud. You're scamming on her boyfriend, and you're scamming on this Buddhist boy now. You know your husband will eventually leave you because you're getting old, and somehow he seems to be getting younger—and you might want to give cooking a try.

"Can't believe you crunched that car. Jesus Christ—there are bound to be cameras, you idiot. It won't be bad enough that you don't have insurance or even that you have to pay for it out of pocket or that everyone's gonna know. But what really burns is that you're not particularly sober. Yes, you're not drunk, and yes, you haven't had a drink in twenty-odd years. But the behavior, hitting and running, especially a fancy car like that, Jesus Christ! What has gotten into you? You might as well drink!"

And the voices didn't stop there:

"Honestly, you got so fat—no wonder that hot Moroccan guy left you, and no wonder you had to settle for the second guy that came along."

And so the voices rang through her head, criticizing, whipping around, tearing her apart. She managed to sit there until she got to the other side, until she got to the flat quiet of moons reflecting on waters, where nothing moved but shimmering liquid and ripples. Where memories were gone, and projections evaporated. Just water, moonlight, and peace, and the closest thing to a giant syringe of heroin that she ever experienced.

She sat that way for about ten minutes and then took a deep breath, put her hands together in a sort of prayer motion, and bowed her head forward.

She stood up from her meditation, took a deep breath, and looked outward instead of in. She imagined that her eyes were glowing, that even the whites were now blue, that she was filled with the Spirit.

She saw him coming back as an adult man, not a diapered boy, and not the type of man he was in the end. He came back at his best. He came back as if he never drank or abused himself, he put his hands on her shoulders, and he looked at her before kissing her gently on the forehead and saying, "There was a reason for all of this, and just because you don't know what that reason is, it does not mean that it is not for the best. Trust me, it will all reveal itself later. It all happened exactly as it was supposed to."

He felt and sounded so real that she simply whispered, "Okay."

She heard her husband's car in the driveway and was glad and excited and couldn't wait for her hug. She had been beaten up by her own mind and the circumstances of her day, and now it was time to be soothed by the company of someone who would not dream of treating her the way she treated herself.

*

The buzzer in the apartment was loud enough that it made certain things on the counter vibrate ever so slightly when it was going off. It gave Jim a start to hear it, and he thought at first that he had a delivery he'd forgotten about. He smiled a little—just a little—at how every single guy who delivered his food always pronounced delivery in the same way: "DeeReeVerrrry."

He got up from the couch and walked slowly out into the hall, wishing he had a video intercom so that he could see who it was before revealing that he was at home. He went into the bedroom and tried to look out of his window down onto Avenue A and 2nd Street, but he still couldn't see in his own entrance on 2nd, and the caller was hidden by the awning.

So he went back into the hall, pressed "Talk,"

and in a calm voice said, "Who is it?"

He let go of the button and quickly heard his sister's voice respond. "Jim, it's me. It's Mary. Let me up."

She was always showing up, always trying too hard for something, always excited. It was almost like she was a girl who liked him—had a crush on him. Someone he didn't like but had to let down easy. She was always following him around, and it irritated him. His own sister, for crying out loud.

And now she was in New York and always dropping by or calling or sending little postcards. Sending postcards when you live in the same city, for crying out loud! And she was only in Midtown, and he was in the East Village, and sometimes it would really irritate him that he loved her but wanted his older sister to be cooler. And he wondered if she was ever going to have a boyfriend or a husband—she was in her thirties now. But it was not like *he* had a girl, and you know it *was* the '80s.

Women could wait—there was no need to rush into relationships—and she had a job that she liked, so who was he to say?

He pressed the talk button. "Hey, Mary, this is kind of a weird time."

He heard back: "Okay, well, I was just passing through, and I have a couple bottles of wine, maybe like four bottles of wine.... Some whites and reds that I have been wanting to try, and I just thought—hell, why not get them and see if I want to buy them again. But I want to try them with somebody.... So, I thought I'd give you a buzz or swing by and see what you're doing before I got on the subway, you know."

He realized that she was nowhere near her subway station. The nearest station was the F train, and she didn't take the F train to go home, so she had come all the way over from the 1 and the 9, which was way over on the other side. She might've taken the L train just to get to his side, but she still would've had to walk all the way down to 2nd Street from 14th Street carrying the wine.

She probably got the wine nearby, at Astor Wines, and she lugged it over, knowing if she had wine or if she had any kind of booze, he would let her up. He felt a deep disgust for her at that moment but didn't even bother saying anything since the disgust was even deeper for himself, because he was willing to give up his evening of solace and quiet—an evening he had planned on not drinking. An evening he had made up his mind about and felt for months sort of comfortable with not drinking, but there was the wine, and there was his sister and the wine was the key to his door, and she knew it.

He pressed the door button and let her up.

He could hear her clamoring up the marble steps. He was on the fourth floor, but it was the fifth really because they didn't count the first floor, which they called the ground floor. The climb was hard for her. She was getting a little heavy around the hips, and he could hear, ever so slightly, the clink of bottles where they had not been wrapped properly with the butcher paper to keep them from smashing.

He felt sick, and he felt mad. She had done this four times in the past two months. Pulling this shit like trying wine or just coming from some imaginary party where she'd say she'd taken half a bottle of whiskey with her and wanted to share it with him before heading back home. Or she had gotten some beers and felt like watching a little bit of the ball game on TV with him. It was always about booze, and she wasn't that big of a drinker. She didn't drink most of it when she got there anyway. She let him drink it all, but in the past month, it seemed like his stomach was getting hard, and it would burn sometimes. His side would hurt and feel puffy and tender to the touch. But it would go away if he drank water for a couple of days.

Sometimes he could go for more than a couple of days just drinking water, and he really felt like maybe one day he could just drink water and stay sober, because he felt like he was a kid again. But then Mary would turn up on the doorstep with the bottles and her need to come up there and chat and just tell him everything that was in her stupid head because she worshiped him.

This was his big sister—he wanted to look up to her, and he just felt like he couldn't. She was as addicted to him as he was to the booze she brought, so there was nothing to look up to—just an odd, repulsive, unspoken contract.

There was a light knock when she reached the front door that he'd left open—but she knocked anyway. He wished she would just walk in, but she was too insecure to even do that.

"It's open. It's open, Mary."

She walked in. She'd gotten herself a little pixie haircut, and her eyes glowed blue even in the dimness of the hallway. His heart sank a level and melted for his sister. He loved her face because it always looked a little worried. She wanted some assurance that he was really happy to see her, but she didn't wait for it in case she didn't get it, so she rushed past into the kitchen, put the bottles down on the counter, and started pulling out the reds and chattering nervously, telling him about the vintage and the country the grapes were stomped in. He just ignored her, went for the opener, and opened one. He got a big glass out, put a glass in front of her, and let her pour her own. Then he just started drinking, knowing that he was going to have to have at least one big drink in him before he could give her the sort of welcome she required. He didn't say anything.

He turned on the TV, and they watched some crap, then a little bit of *Happy Days*, some reruns or something, a little bit of Reagan talking about something or other, and they just sat there and drank.

He finished off two bottles pretty quickly. The

last two he went a bit slower, and Mary started to fall asleep. He told her she could stay there. They had had one deep conversation about love and whether it really existed, and she teared up. He told her she could sleep in the spare room where his desk was, where he was supposed to be writing his great American novel, his own big science fiction book that he hadn't even made a start on.

It cost you money to stall the dream you weren't working to pursue. Instead of writing, he'd look outside at the hookers and the junkies in the street. He'd wonder how long it would be before he would be down in the streets with them. He wondered how many times he would tell Mary to come on up with the booze. He wondered if he would ever tell her to go away, if he would ever let her come up and just drink it all herself while he watched or if he could ever ask her:

"What the hell do you do this for? Why do you bribe me with alcohol? Why do you try and get my love? Do you do this consciously, or is it just unconscious? Do you know the only reason you're of any interest to me tonight is because you came bearing alcohol? If you know this about me, and you can love me anyway, and you know this about you, and you can live with yourself anyway, which one of us is sick? Which one of us is sicker?"

*

One of the saddest things about Mary's desire to be with her little brother at any cost, even if it meant plying him with alcohol, was that, when he did get drunk, he was slightly abusive or one might just call it emotionally unkind to her.

It wasn't so that one could call it abuse, but there was certainly a picking apart of her and who she was that he did very readily and comfortably once he had a few glasses of wine and was on his fourth cigarette. He would slouch down in his chair in the apartment with all the noise of the avenue whizzing by, and he would look over at Mary and find in himself perhaps a certain annoyance at her relief that she had won and was comfortable and happy because she got what she wanted, got to be with her brother. He would look at himself and the fact that he was drunk yet again and see it as being her fault, but he knew deep down that it was his own fault for not being able to say no. And all of this was too much to think about and too much to speak of, so he would change the subject, and the undertone of anger would infiltrate whatever it was that the new subject would be. He would suddenly ask:

"Mary, why don't you have a boyfriend? You know, maybe you can go and dye out some of that new gray you've got. You're much too young to have gray hair. And now, I know Mom got gray hair early, but hey, you don't have to."

Or:

"You know, all these pegged jeans are in and

everything, but I don't know if they're really right for your body type. Well, maybe with a big shirt. Or one of those cut-off sweatshirts with one shoulder showing."

Or:

"Mary, you're a handsome woman. What are you hiding from? What are you afraid of?"

Mary's heart would sink and pound all at once when he would start up like this, and she would take it seriously and try to avert the full assaults. She'd change the subject and laugh nervously, and that seemed to only make him want to hurt her more.

He hated her cowardice. He hated her when she was afraid of him, and he hated how much she loved him despite that fear.

So her eyes would well up a little, and he would see this and say, "Oh, honey, come on, come on. I'm your brother. I'm just trying to help." And she would say, "I know, I know, I know," and pretend that she really didn't mind. And they would move on and often talk about other people and skewer their characters, but eventually, by the sixth glass of wine, maybe the seventh, he would ask another question:

"So, Mary, what's the deal with your work? Like is this your passion? Is this your bliss, or is it something you're doing so that you have money because you're afraid of not having money?"

This was the other area where he would try to humiliate her—or, at least, she felt humiliated. Her need for bills to be paid. He mocked her need for order, and yet if it wasn't for her having a job and having money, a lot of his bills would not get paid either. He had a pseudo-artist's disdain for the working world, and yet he was always broke and wanted to borrow money that she could only get by working for it.

The only thing left to do for Mary was to join him and drink past her comfort zone. The third glass, that changed her and sent her into another character in another place. She changed from an enabler to someone who could run with him through the fields of ridiculousness and full-blown inebriation.

And more and more in order to feel okay, she had to drink past the third glass, whether she was with him or whether she wasn't.

More and more when she wasn't with him and with other people or with friends of her own, she would take on his character and emulate him and let them play the part of weak little Mary with her skirt dragging in the dirt. And so she would pretend to be him, and she would drink like him and take on his questioning tone, and she would assume the character of her own brother around people who did not know him, and she would become mean, boastful, and bullying.

That is when she knew what it was like to be him. That is when she would know what it was like to not be afraid of him by living inside him when he was not there and drinking as much as him. And when she was with him, drinking as much as him kept her from feeling the full scorn of his wrath. Pretty soon, only three glasses of wine seemed absurd—for children, cowards, and little baby girls who were afraid of everything.

And that's how it began. That's how she took over where he left off. The sicker he got and the less he could drink, the more she drank for him, and the quieter he got, the more chatty she became. Ultimately, when he died she lived on instead of him.

She applied for jobs that she thought he might have gotten. She told women all about him—women who she thought would have fallen in love with her brother. And a part of her became him.

But this part of him that she carried inside her long after his death, long after she had gotten sober in the rooms of twelve-step programs—for him and for herself—this personality of his lived inside her, and frequently it needed a body so that she could talk to it to keep her company.

It was not enough that it was simply an entity in her head that conversed with her. She would find people who were just blank enough to embody him and just similar enough to be believable. They were generally young men about the age her brother was when he died. He would've been much older by this time, of course, but in her mind's eye, he needed to be a certain age. He needed to be no more than thirty-five, and he needed to be alcoholic, but he needed to recover the way her brother might've if he had stopped drinking and not turned his two livers into cottage cheese.

And then she would pursue her strategy of impressing these men—these "friends," these people she would do huge favors for, whose projects she would take under her wing or finance, and then she would find some solace and some relief from the constant pain, from the constant blipping of hospital machines in her head. The nonstop sounds of machines as it all went to shit—as he died right under them, as they didn't do their job or were taxed and could not do any more than they were designed to.

He got to live in her and, through her, he got to live in the bodies of other men, and she still in some way or other, instead of delivering wine to people's front doors as she did for her brother to get him to be her friend, she delivered favors to the front doors of these young men, until their wives or their girlfriends or boyfriends grew uncomfortable and would say to their men:

"You know that she's bribing you? She is bribing you for your friendship or for whatever it is that she needs. You know that she has her own husband. Why is she calling here and being this intimate with you, sweetheart? I understand she's old enough to be your mother, but it's still not cool. Get rid of her."

And they would.

Other people knew this about her, but she did not. Other people felt ill at ease with this strange shadow play, but she was too enmeshed herself. The puppets that she put in place—playing her brother in the '80s in New York and whatever else that she herself was quite oblivious to—were eventually automatic and always futile. It never ended happily but always petered out or abruptly stopped. She simply felt empty and strange, and she would go home and let her husband hold her like he was her daddy, and she'd fall asleep, sometimes crying with no ability to explain why.

*

Something about that environment, all the young women around she knew she would no longer be competing with, at least overtly made her want to cultivate her nurturing side. The idea of being a den mother suddenly seemed like a safe way to be. To be needed without being in the cold breeze of competition and without being in the harsh storm of hanging on to youth, when it was all done, sometimes after a while a woman could really find herself.

When she first started going to the meetings, going to twelve-step programs, she would watch the women. She would watch them gather round one older woman after the meeting or one or two sort of married matrons—the types who were smiling and laughing, petting the young women's hair, listening to them intently, handing out phone numbers, being like mothers. She remembered seeing this and wondering how it was that it had never occurred to her that perhaps she could relate to another woman in the role of helper and sponsor, and how it was that she had never understood the beauty of the thing. And, of course, the reason was because she had had no female relatives—not even her own mother.

Most women she knew were her teachers: people to admire or fear or ones her own age she felt she had to compete with. But with time, there were shifts in dynamics, and the women who were considered adults were younger and younger as she grew older and older. And more and more it seemed like it was time for her to cultivate that granny side, that kind side that made you safe to men and other women and children, and occasionally animals too.

So the years passed, and she took on various sponsors and sponsees, trying to emulate how the older women treated people, and she treated her sponsees in the same way too.

And with time, her hair grew white, and she was able to fill that role a lot more, visually, if not completely with her heart. She did become a matron as her hips filled out in a way that they had never been before. She had been a hippie person but not like this—her breasts flattened somewhat, her skin became mapped with little veins, and there was now some white in her eyebrows, and even her voice changed; it had a little crack in it.

Girls approached her more comfortably after meetings. They wanted her to play the role, they wanted her to be the mother, but somehow she found herself falling more easily into the brittle teacher role. And there was a certain kind of girl, a certain kind of clever intellectual girl, who didn't want to be mothered, who wanted to have a mentor she could admire. Those types found her more and more. They were not huggers or cuddlers; they were not the type of sweet girls who took her advice and just wanted to come by and bring cookies. They were anti-girls.

But they wore her out and called her on her unintentional games. She wished she could draw girls who looped their arms into hers and rubbed her shoulders. She envied the love that passed between the younger women and the older ones, as opposed to the strange brisk professional hostility she had with her sponsees.

As she gave up trying to care about women, she gave them assessments of who they were and how they could change in order to be righteous and spiritual warriors, and so on and so forth. She regurgitated what her Buddhist teachers had taught her in all the books she had piled up and all the self-help nonsense that filled her head.

But with the men—with the men that she made friends—with the gay men, the young married men, the men who were not threatened by her so they had no idea that she was actually getting off on the acquaintance—the men who would never think of her sexually so it never occurred to them that to her it was an affair—it was about the intimacy and about them turning to her for a sort of love that only she could give. She could only mindlessly let them be sick and make them sicker, only mindlessly let them go uncorrected and tell them, "You are fine just the way you are. Don't let the bastards get you down." Making herself indispensable, whether through motherly or sisterly acts or simply comradely behavior—the way a man looked at her when he felt this way about her—it was her drug.

The truth was she had never been that big on alcohol like her brother had been. She should have taken herself to the meetings for the friends and families of alcoholics. She could have gone to learn that the drunk in the family eventually becomes what everyone else is addicted to.

But she wanted to be part of the bravado of the drunks. She wanted to be closer to the drinkers. She didn't want to be in the group you joined if you'd been a hanger-on—the groupie program.

She didn't want to get better. She felt she was just fine. It was everyone else.

Once in a while, she would catch a glimpse of herself in the window of the meeting room in the church or rec center, and it would usually be dark outside so the windows would turn into mirrors, and she would be startled. She would see her own body language, flirtatious, but in a subtle way, difficult for anyone to pinpoint. It was as if she was being gentle and kind and funny and young-spirited—not flirtatious, exactly. Then she would see herself and look at her hips pressing against the sides of her jeans where they had faded from the flesh rubbing, and she would feel something beyond shame. Something ridiculous, something akin to hearing her brother sneering.

That was it—her brother would laugh at her if he could see her there right then. Was this whole thing supposed to be just a way to win his approval? She knew deep down he would mock everything she was doing anyway. From being in a program to trying to help women and pretending to want to help men. His bullshit detector would fly into the stratosphere, and he would say:

"Mary! Who are you kidding? What the fuck life is this? Why do you need to be needed so badly? Why are you so weak? Why are you always hiding your agendas and your motives? Just be yourself…. Just be alone and read a book. You always look around to see what everyone thinks of you. It is so difficult to be around you, and it's impossible to love you, because you need too much."

Yes, that's exactly what he would say. She no longer was sure if these were things he had actually said or if she knew him so well that even after his death, he lived on in her brain and still generated sentences and thoughts. His personality was renting space inside her head and heckling her life's idiotic performance.

Chapter Five

The Sex Addict

"MY NAME IS DICK, and I am a sex addict."

"Hi, Dick."

"Hey, everyone. It's good to be at a meeting, and I feel grateful that I have a solution today and don't have to act out and do the things that used to hurt me so much. Thank you, Jack, for asking me to speak today. I'm glad there's no particular format at this meeting, because I think I might be a little bit all over the place. What I'm dealing with today is the sort of thing that would drive me to download porn on the Internet for hours or get a hooker or have some sort of inappropriate sexual thing with a woman. But today, I can open up about my pain and sadness.... Really talk about what is hurting me instead of hurting myself on top of the hurt that's there already."

The circle of men nodded. They were in a church rectory in a hip part of Los Angeles. They wore shorts and jeans, and most sat on their folded metal chairs with their legs spread or ankles crossed on knees. They wore serious expressions of knowingness and depth. There was an undertow of anger in the room, a vibration in the key of the wronged.

Something felt coiled and ready to spring. The man speaking had a long, gray ponytail. He was in his forties and articulated his words in a way that the others in the room took to signify education. Some knew that he was a person of standing in the community, maybe a media figure or something, a respected social type who knew about art and politics or knew people who knew about art and politics.

"I'm dealing with some grief that I keep thinking will pass. It's been three years, but I'm still sorting through the betrayal that seems to really stay alive for me. I think many of us have been betrayed, and I know I'm not unique in how difficult it is to get over that. So I'll just tell you the story and see if there is some healing in that or if my experience can help someone else.

"About three years ago, I had to come to terms with the fact that I had a problem with sex. I was engaged to a beautiful and successful woman whom I loved more than anything, and we lived in a beautiful home surrounded by our wonderful friends and family. I had just been through a very difficult family issue, and this woman had stayed by my side, and we were closer and more in love than ever.

"But at night, after she fell asleep, I'd get up and look at porn and go on chat rooms online. I'd hook up with women on my lunch break whom I'd met online the night before and have sex in motels. I'd pay prostitutes for sex in our own home when my fiancée was away on business.

"This double life was eating me up, so I sought out help from a therapist who sent me to you guys. My saviors! It was here that it was explained to me that I'm not scum and that I don't have a moral problem. What I have is a disease. I can't help that I have this disease, but through hard work and a belief in a higher power, I can at least have a daily reprieve from this devastating and baffling sex addiction.

"So I got a sponsor and did the steps and abstained from all addictive behavior for two months, but it became clear that I had to come clean and tell my fiancée the truth. I loved her so much, and everything I did to clean up my act and get well was for her. I felt that if I told her she would see me through—join me, and we would get through this together. It was in some ways our disease, since I sometimes felt like she knew something was up and was covering up for me—for us."

The men in the circle nodded especially hard when the speaker mentioned the concept of "us," of getting through the sexual infidelities with the person who had been cheated on. The speaker paused and nodded back at the men, a simpatico moment and a sort of springboard for whatever tragic outcome he was preparing his listeners for. His voice had slowly worked its way into an on-air pitch or a sort of fast-food drive-through-order voice.

"So the day came, and I talked to my sponsor

and prayed and then told my fiancée that we had to talk. I sat her down in our living room, took a deep breath, and told her everything. It took a few hours, but I left nothing out. I told her about every single porn site, every hooker, every Craigslist casual encounter. I pulled no punches, and I'll tell you I've never cried so hard in my life, nor have I felt closer to another human being.

"She said nothing.... She listened, and the room got dark as the sun started to set. She twisted the beautiful engagement ring I had spent thousands of dollars on and surprised her with in the funniest, most romantic way you can imagine—every girl's dream—the way I gave her that ring. She twisted and twisted the ring, then she'd hold her head and shake it once in a while. Then I told her about my recovery, how I was clean and how I was committed to recovery, and that she could go to support meetings too to deal with her feelings about the disease that had affected us, this sex addiction—all its victims needed to get help. I told her that we would get through it.... I didn't say it would be easy. There would be setbacks and relapses, but we'd always get back on track now that we knew what it was that we were dealing with.

"So she finally spoke and asked me how long it had been going on. I told her, about six years. We'd been together for about seven years. Then she asked how long since I had been clean and I told her two months. I sort of look back now and wonder what she was calculating in her head. I still can't figure it out. She was thirty-three at the time, and I know that's not really young anymore for women, so they think about time a lot. But anyway, that's all she asked, and then she said she needed some time to digest this stuff and would be staying at a friend's house that night and would see me the next day. "I got scared but happy too. She was trying to process it, and her behavior was so mature. She didn't yell or break anything. I wasn't in the "doghouse," and she didn't try to tell me what to do.... 'Cause you know how much we hate that."

The room nodded again at that last sentence. Somehow they had a collective and visceral hatred for anything that resembled being told what to do. They were all transfixed by the story as it reached its end. A sort of hush fell over the room the way it does when very little girls are awaiting the happiest part of their princess bedtime story—the part where the princess is saved by the prince and removed from her unfortunate lot in life by some fantastic twist of fate and through no action of her own. Little girls and cheaters respond with profound emotion to such stories of passive salvation.

"So she left and said she'd call me in the morning at my work, but I didn't hear from her all day, and she didn't pick up her cell. When I called her job they said she had called in sick. But I said the serenity prayer and showed up for my responsibilities at work until it was time to go home.

"And this is the part of the story where I just fall apart, so please excuse me.... I'm crying some very old tears before you.

"I got home, and as I opened the door, I got the worst shock of my life. I walked in, and everything was gone. All the furniture and all her clothes, even the wine. She had bought an amazing wine collection, which I'd selected for her bottle by bottle and stored perfectly. She didn't know anything about wine, and I opened her up to that world. That collection was as much mine as hers.

"She even took the dog and every photograph with herself in it. It was like she had never existed. There was no note or anything.

"I called her friends and family, and the only person who would talk to me was her father. This big Midwestern man who has been married to the same woman for forty years and has never left his hometown and knows nothing about the world told me straight up that I was dead to all of them and to stay away from his daughter. That fucking hillbilly got to talk down to me! Sorry, sorry, that is my hurt talking! God bless the man. I pray for him to get everything he wants.

"But she'd told everyone.... Everyone she knew thought I was a pig and a cheat. She hadn't even had the common decency to protect me or to be discreet about something that was my business. I guess it was her business too, but she left me, so she was just being vengeful. Hell hath no fury, et cetera, et cetera. She abandoned me, and I have not seen her since."

The men in the circle sat wide-eyed and horrified. They shook their heads in admonishment of the selfish woman who had so let down one of their own. Many covered their mouths as if to stifle screams of fear. Many had experienced the same letdown. Others lived in fear of it.

The speaker wiped his moist, red face with the wad of tissues someone had passed around to him. He took a deep breath of relief and fanned his face with a passing but unusually feminine gesture, and then he forced a brave smile.

"But it's okay. She is in my prayers too. She isn't on the same spiritual path as I am. She will have to deal with her lack of forgiveness and judgment, and she has her own higher power. Still, there are days when I think about it and can't help how upset and obsessed I get. I heard a song today. The chorus of the song was, "You are forgiven, you are forgiven, you are forgiven." Three godly words that just brought me to tears. I thought about my fiancée and how none of her friends or colleagues will tell me anything about her. I've been told by my sponsor not to google her or try to find her, and that has certainly made me wonder if I need a new sponsor, since I think it's my right to have closure. But that's another share.

"I wonder what she's doing. If she found some other guy to jump into bed with right away. If she's married or something. All I know is that it could have been amazing for us. She's thirty-six now, but she was so beautiful when she was young, and I would have done everything to keep her happy. But she threw it all away, and I have to find some way to deal with my resentment towards her for what she did to me. I have to be the one to forgive.

"So that's it from me today, folks. I'd really like to turn the meeting back over to the room and hear from you guys."

The room erupted in applause. Some of the men in the circle were crying too, and some simply clapped hard and slow, nodding and calling out, "Keep coming back, man, keep coming back!"

• **Chapter Six** •

Nelly

WHEN SHE HAD BEEN ABOUT THIRTEEN, her mother had taken her to the dentist to figure out what to do about her three crooked bottom teeth. It was there that the dentist had suggested they break her jaw or give her some sort of chin implant to fix the weak recession at the bottom of her otherwise passable face. She did have nice blue eyes, and although her nose was fleshy and undefined, it was straight. A strengthening chin implant could have really balanced it all out.

Nelly was proud of recounting the story of her reaction to her mother actually considering the dentist's suggestion that her daughter have her face reconstructed.

"I screamed at her, 'How could you listen to that bastard? You are horrible! You should think I'm perfect the way I am. How dare he suggest I need to have my face fucked with!'"

It was true that Nelly's strong sense of self as a child was admirable and that her mother had been a touch thoughtless, but the real point of pride for Nelly in the scenario seemed to involve how thoroughly she had shamed and belittled her own mother. She often talked about how frustrating her mother's mealy-mouthed indifference was and how frequently she had to scream at her about her cluelessness and lack of savvy. Nelly would quickly point out that her mother was, of course, her best friend—"Don't get me wrong"—but she could just be so stupid. Nelly would chastise her mother for the woman's generosity to anyone other than herself and wonder out loud how her father could continue to dote on such a spaced-out fool.

Nelly fought regularly for what she felt were her rights. When she brought her expensive lingerie to work and washed it in the communal washer, then found that they had been dried improperly by someone who thought they were being helpful, she made such a stink about it that her boss ended up lying to production and saying that the underwear had been part of an actor's costume and that the whole load had been destroyed so they would have to repurchase hundreds of dollars' worth of thongs. Nelly felt satisfied but still angry at the inconvenience. Even though her underwear had not been destroyed, tumble-drying them had taken serious time out of the lifespan of the elastic. Nelly did not feel that it was partly her own responsibility for having left the items in the washer for six hours—a washer that was not even intended for personal use but for crew members to clean and maintain the actors' costumes.

Even after Nelly got her money and her way, however, she clung to an outrage about the incident and a profound hatred for all the people who might have been the ones to put her wash in the dryer for her.

"Even if they had taken it out and not dried it, even if they had just put the wash on top of the dryer, they would have been wrong. They have no right to touch my things. They should have had someone get on the walkie-talkie and find out whose wash it was."

Nelly's heart would beat rapidly and uncomfortably every time she thought about the incident. She found herself thinking of it over and over, bringing it up to her boss, who by now had found herself also joining in the outrage, if for no other reason than to not end up on the wrong end of Nelly's convictions.

Nelly took good care of her things. She bought quality things. She liked nice things. She enjoyed perfection and sleek design. When the married man she had dated went back to his wife, Nelly took consolation in how much weight she lost from being too upset to eat. She felt stronger and more streamlined in her expensive new clothes.

She lived in a studio apartment that was more like a storage unit and launching pad than a home. But to look at her, you could just imagine the sort of home she coveted and believed she deserved. Home was where the heart was. Nelly did not need one of her own but believed it would be given to her.

One July afternoon, she took a single pair of rather pricey pants to her local dry cleaner in West Hollywood. She put it in a plastic bag and decided to try out the establishment down the street—they could surely clean a pair of pants. Although she usually sent her dry cleaning along with the actors' clothes on whatever TV show she was working on, she was not currently on a job, so the free perks were unavailable.

She walked into the shop, and the first thing she saw was a sign that surprised her. It read: "If dry cleaning is not picked up within thirty days of drop-off date, dry cleaner will dispose of the item. Please be responsible and retrieve your clothes. We do not have the space to store your cleaning."

Nelly didn't like ultimatums and felt irked by the tone of the sign, but at the same time, she knew that she herself would be enraged if someone left their crap in her car and didn't come to get it. She had on more than one occasion thrown out little things people forgot at her work. Not the principal actors, but the extras—the ones who were not famous and were always making problems she had to deal with. If one of them left their sweater or something, she would toss it in the trash instead of bothering to ask the office to put it in a lost-and-found box.

So, even though the sign gave her pause, she saw the reason behind it and proceeded to go to the counter and hand in her pants.

She was told that it would cost $6.22 to have the pants dry-cleaned. She felt that was reasonable and handed them over. The Asian woman writing out the dry-cleaning ticket read back Nelly's name, irritating her by pronouncing it "Nerry." Nelly felt compelled to correct her:

"Nelly, not Nerry."

The woman just looked at her. So she grabbed the ticket from her hand and walked out, heading back to her apartment.

Some time passed, perhaps a week or two, and Nelly remembered the pants and how she had to go back and get them. But things had picked up at work, as she'd been called back in at the TV show she so liked. Upon returning to the job, she found that one of her colleagues had taken a few days off, and in her absence, Nelly began to ingratiate herself with the people she'd watched the absent girl consort with. She was determined to land a full-time position on the show and did whatever she could to make that possible.

The secondary boss was behind her—the very same one who had lied for her and reimbursed her for the not-damaged items in the lingerie incident. This boss seemed to enjoy Nelly's company in some ways. Nelly knew how to make herself indispensable to the woman. She would bring her little gifts, pastries, and set gossip. She would say "yes" when instructed, in a quick way while bowing her head. She was good at pretending to be servile. The girl who was absent for a few days, on the other hand, behaved towards the boss like an equal. She did not fake servility, nor did she throw her weight around, but she didn't make an impression either, not on somebody like the boss, who only registered extremes.

So Nelly grew busy with her ambition. She had noticed that the absent woman remembered everyone's names, so Nelly began carrying a small notebook to write down everybody's names in, and she made sure to use their names when saying hello. The prop master, the key grip, whoever. She decided that it must be important to use their names, that somehow the absent woman had gotten results on the job with this technique and people seemed to like her. People asked where she was when she wasn't around. It did not occur to Nelly that it was not a tactic, that the absent woman naturally enjoyed knowing people and thus was liked in return.

More time passed, and it was finally about five weeks since she had dropped off her pants at the cleaners.

They would have theme days in the wardrobe department at her work, and that Friday's theme was going to be the show *Dynasty*. The high-waisted slacks she had dropped off at the cleaners seemed perfect for that late-'80s look, and they would go well with a retro shoulder-padded blazer.

So midweek, she got off work early and headed

back to the dry cleaner to get her pants. She held out the ticket to the woman at the counter, the same woman who had taken the pants from her. The woman looked at the ticket without taking it and looked back at Nelly blankly.

It was strange. It was as if, with all the customers and clothes that the dry cleaner had, she had somehow remembered this one customer and this particular pair of pants and didn't even need to check the rack. She simply looked at Nelly and said:

"It's five weeks. We throw away after thirty day."

Nelly stared back in disbelief.

"What?"

"We throw away pants."

"You did what?"

"You were late. We keep thirty days. It's been five week. We throw away pants."

"What the fuck are you talking about? What do you mean you throw away pants? You threw away my fucking $300 pants? You better go back there and fucking find them, that's what you better do, or you better write me a check!"

"That is policy. We have sign. We throw away after thirty day. You gone five weeks."

"I don't know what the fuck you're talking about, but I'm gonna come back tomorrow, and I'm gonna fucking have my pants."

"We no have pants. We throw away. You leave now."

Nelly was visibly crazed. She had been banging her fist on the counter during the exchange while pointing with her other hand and speaking in a voice that was so loud it was close to a scream. So she just kept on screaming:

"You dumb whore! You stupid Chinese whore!" The woman pointed to the door and just said:

"Get out. Get out of my store."

Nelly walked out. She went home and raged. She was sweating, her heart was pounding, and she didn't know what to do. She thought she was going to lose her mind.

"They have to have my pants. They have to have my pants. They don't have the right. I'm going to get my fucking pants."

She decided to call a few people. Mostly these were male friends who were not really available for friendship anymore and seemed to not be checking their voicemails. But one guy, Bill, who had a high school crush on her, always tried to be available for Nelly's venting upsets.

Bill had let her talk him into being her writing partner—she wanted to sell a script. She'd seen how many people just wrote them and sold them, and she wanted in on the action. But she couldn't write and needed someone who could. Although Bill could write, Nelly grew tired of him and his inability to take her suggestions and follow her very clear instructions. For one thing, he was poor and wouldn't call LA during the day, always waiting until after nine at night, when it was free on his cell phone. His complete lack of coolness made it impossible to count on him to network in New York and further their still-unwritten project.

Bill wasn't stupid. He knew Nelly was trying to use him, so he wouldn't do what she wanted but continued to pretend to be her writing partner and let her berate him once in a while. He did this just to stay in touch, and he always listened whenever she needed someone to listen.

So she called New York, he picked up at his job and, after a few adjustments, was able to find an empty conference room where he could to listen to her. She ranted and raved and ranted and raved for at least twenty-five minutes about her pants, until Bill finally said:

"Why didn't you just pick them up?"

This question enraged her even more, and she started yelling at him.

"Oh, you're blaming me because they lost my pants? Because they stole my pants? Some stupid fat fuck is probably wearing my pants, and you're blaming me? That's like blaming someone who got raped. What do you mean, why didn't I pick up my pants? 'Cause I don't have to. Why should I? I'm the customer."

"All right, all right. Jesus Christ, Nelly, why don't you just calm down? Have a glass of wine or something."

"You know what? You know what, Bill? I gotta go. I just feel like everything for you is a joke, and you've got your shitty job, and you say you want to write this script, but you don't want to actually have to do the work, you just want me to do it, and you can't even really listen to me when I need a friend. Fuck you and goodbye."

Nelly hung up the phone. Bill listened in stunned amazement to the dial tone and then hung up too. He didn't know why he stayed friends with her. His girlfriend hated her, and deep down, so did he. He didn't know why he had liked her in high school. She had a weird face, sort of cartoony, with no chin, buckteeth, and a bulbous nose. She had always been slender, which was nice. In high school, she had been a sort of higher grade of nerd. She could have almost been one of the popular kids, and she seemed to be always planning her way out of her low status in the social world of high school. And that made her interesting—the fact that she felt she had a chance on the other side. She had something, and he wanted to know what it was.

Whatever it was, it took her to Hollywood. Whatever it was, it landed her a job in show business. Somehow he didn't have that, and he wished he knew how to get it. Maybe it was the capacity for outrage about a pair of pants. Maybe it was the capacity to buy a pair of $300 pants. He could never buy a pair of $300 pants. He'd never dare give himself the right. And that's how it was—that's how things were for him. He couldn't do it. So he knew he would call back later and apologize, and he knew that the lopsided friendship would go on as long as Nelly needed it to. He didn't know what would happen after that.

Nelly paced in her studio apartment, back and forth, back and forth. She thought about the pants; she thought about her rent. She thought about how, if she paid $300 extra for rent instead of for pants or for Manolo Blahnik shoes or Gucci sunglasses, she could probably afford a one-bedroom, but that didn't matter to her. Whatever extra money she was going to make she was going to use to lease a BMW. She kept thinking about all the things she deserved, all the things she worked to get, like her lingerie that somebody abused and threw in the dryer, like her $300 pants that somebody took for granted and stole or threw away or lost.

"Who are these people? Who are these losers in the world who are always trying to take my things? Who are they? I'm gonna get those fucking pants if it's the last fucking thing I do, and that dry cleaner doesn't even know who she's fucking with."

She sat back in her easy chair, got on the Internet, and researched everything she could about possible litigation, about suing the cleaners, and she did this until two in the morning, when she grew weary and fell asleep in the chair at first, then stumbled into her bed only a few feet away. She had to be at work by six the next day. She tossed and turned and dreamed about punching and kicking and scratching. She dreamed about shooting and about being shot. She did not sleep well.

The next day at work, Nelly told every single person who would listen about the pants, and every single person, uniformly, shared her outrage, but instead of this sympathy being soothing to Nelly, every time somebody sided with her, she would grow more and more agitated. She came close to leaving work—just to go back to the store to yell at the dry cleaner some more. She kept stopping different people at work, people she barely knew or had little occasion to talk to, and told them what happened and asked them what she should do. And they would say:

"You should go back there and get your pants or tell them they have to pay you back. They have to pay for the pants. They have to pay to get you new ones."

So that's how the day went, and the angrier she got, the more she felt that justice was being served. She felt that if she let her anger ebb even slightly or stopped being outraged for a moment, justice would be abandoned, and terrible abuses would go unchecked. And so she burned all day, nervously chewing on things, playing and replaying her conversation with the dry cleaner and editing her mind's movie of the event into versions where she won, or the dry cleaner was disrespectful, and Nelly defended herself and fought back.

The more she worked herself up, the more she would snap and yell at the background artists she had to dress. She gave a vicious tongue-lashing to one man for spilling cranberry juice on his shirt, saying, "What are you? Retarded?" Another background artist jumped in and defended him, to which Nelly squealed:

"Don't you defend him. Mind your own business, or I'll send you home as well."

One of the assistant directors took Nelly aside and told her that the guy who had spilled the juice was mentally handicapped, and even if he wasn't it would be better to not use words like "retarded." Nelly stared at the assistant director in amazement and burst out laughing:

"God, I can't believe I did that! He's really retarded?"

The AD just shook his head and walked away. Wardrobe was known for being a callous department of idiotic, angry folk, but this Nelly, the AD observed, was especially bad. And yet, on some days, she could be quite charming, quite funny, and so you could forgive her. But when he saw her talk to the poor handicapped man, that was when he knew who she really was.

By the time she left work, after a fifteen-hour day, the dry cleaner was closed, but she went and stood outside the store anyway. It was dark, with traffic rushing by to home or wherever. The bakery next door and all the other places that created foot traffic were closed. She was the only pedestrian out. It seemed to her that everything closed early on her particular block of West Hollywood.

She stood and just stared through the shop window and thought how good it would feel to find a brick and throw it through the glass or to take gasoline and a match and torch the place. She imagined telling the dry cleaning woman how she hoped someone would do that to her shop—not implicating herself, but saying she hoped someone else would do it. And then, when the place would burn down and the brick would be found inside, the dry cleaning lady would shudder in fear and awe, knowing it had been Nelly but not able to prove it. Nelly imagined with orgasmic pleasure the smile she would give the woman over her shoulder as she walked by the rubble and passed the fire trucks. And the woman would wish she had never lost Nelly's pants. The fantasy made Nelly feel as close to ecstasy as was possible without narcotic assistance.

Nelly pulled her jacket closer around herself, hugging her shoulders as if it was cold, although it was an especially warm evening. The Santa Anas were blowing from the surface of the hot fire in Nelly's mind, like the strange searing breeze that escapes when you open an oven. A balmy eighty degrees, strange for an LA night.

She stared at her reflection in the glass and imagined herself flying like a ghost, thinning and becoming transparent so that she could get into the shop through the crack of the door. She imagined herself, having entered, wafting into the back of the store and flipping through the racks of dry cleaning and finding her pants. Holding them in her hands once more and knowing somehow that the cleaner's young daughter had been wearing the pants and had begun to alter them because she was shorter than Nelly. She had begun to alter the pants, cutting the expensive fabric at the cuffs, destroying the long, lean design so she could put the pants on her stubby thieving legs. Nelly imagined catching the girl in the act, ripping the pants out of her hands and choking her with them, saying, "I got you—you think you can pull one over on me? Well, you can't."

She stood on the sidewalk and stared at the door and her own reflection some more. The cut of her jacket caught her eye. It was a nice design; she'd paid about $500 for it, and she felt that it was worth it. She felt that it was important to pay more money for an item she could have for a long time, and that was made well.

She thought about the other girls at work— some of the makeup girls had no idea who the important new designers were. They were still wearing that crap Juicy Couture, which was never cool. Crap made in China. She would look them up and down and think they looked cheap and stupid.

Satisfied even more with her jacket after thinking of the crap other people wore, she pulled the collar up and felt it brush against her chin.

She liked her chin, her weak chin.

"Who's weak now, fucker?" she hissed out loud and walked back to her apartment.

The next day, Nelly got up for work with enough time to go down to the bakery and get a coffee and croissant. She stood outside the bakery with her breakfast, not wanting to commit to sitting down, since she didn't have that kind of time. She stood and chewed her pastry and thought about what she was going to say when she went next door to the dry cleaner.

She'd stayed up most of the night thinking about very calm, cool, collected things that she could say, plain, slow, and understandable to foreigners.

She finished her food but not her coffee, deciding she didn't need two free hands and that having a drink with her made her seem more casual, like her visit was incidental.

The bell on the dry cleaner's door tingled when she opened it. As soon as Nelly walked in, the Asian woman behind the counter saw her and began to yell.

Nelly froze and watched the shopkeeper waving her arms in their blue smock sleeves. Nelly hadn't been prepared for the possibility that the woman too may have lain awake thinking about their altercation and was ready to react to another visit.

"You get out! You get out! You crazy! You get out!"

Nelly's whole calm plan went out the window as soon as the woman called her crazy. Who did she think she was, calling her that?

Nelly took two big steps up to the counter and proceeded to yell back—things she herself couldn't understand. Her hand came flying down onto the countertop, and the coffee it held ejected its plastic sip lid and went flying up like a rock had been dropped into it from a great height. As the coffee splattered the woman and the walls and the floor, Nelly screamed:

"Look what you've done! Look what you made me do! You fucking bitch! You better find my pants, or I want a check for $358, then I want you to tack on another $300 for the emotional distress you've put me through. I want you to find my pants, and I'm gonna come back tomorrow, and I'm gonna get my fucking pants. You better have them. I hope someone puts a brick through your window. I hope somebody burns this place down."

The woman behind the counter grew very still when she heard the last exclamations about bricks and flames. The idea made her stop. She took a deep breath and said to Nelly:

"We close. Business close. We go out of business."

Nelly looked around and finally saw the new signs stating that it was the shop's last week of business. She began to shake her head, sure that this was a ploy to get away with keeping her pants.

"Oh, no, you fucking don't close with my pants.... With my money! I'm coming back tomorrow, and you better have a check. No—I don't want your check, it's fucking gonna bounce. I want cash. Have my pants or have some cash."

Nelly grabbed her nearly empty coffee, leaving behind puddle and lid on the counter. She walked out and tried to unsuccessfully slam the door—it was on a hydraulic hinge that slowed it down, but the bell rung frantically.

Nelly walked to her fully paid-off car—her economical car, which was embarrassing enough to her for its lack of luxury, but it had also given her nothing but trouble. She got into the car and slammed her fists on the steering wheel.

"I'm going to fucking get rid of you. I'm sick of pouring money into your piece of shit engine. I deserve better than this. I'm gonna get my fucking BMW—you just wait and see. You'll all fucking see."

Nelly looked quite nice that day. She wore a T-shirt dress with a thick belt and well-cobbled flats that she had bought in a few different colors since she never knew when she'd find a good pair of shoes she liked again.

Nelly drove to work at top speed. She loved speed and imagined how much faster she could drive in the new car she'd get.

Her music was blaring, so the cop car must have been behind her whirring his siren for a while before she heard him and saw the flashing lights at the same time. She just couldn't believe it. She pulled over and waited to be asked if she knew how fast she was driving in a thirty-five-miles-per-hour zone. She knew she'd been going sixty but was prepared to innocently state that she thought she was driving at the speed limit.

Two policemen approached from the cop car and headed towards her vehicle. She was very close to work and prepared to make the whole thing end as fast as possible. She pulled down the front of her dress before they reached her car, making her already low-cut top lower. She felt confident that having perky breasts was enough to distract the idiotic men in blue.

"Driver's license and registration, please. Do you know how fast you were going?"

The cop speaking to her seemed amicable, while his frowning partner took out his notepad and began to write.

"I think I was going thirty-five or forty?"

The amicable cop walked back to the squad car to run her license and registration while the frowning cop stayed behind. His hair was pitch-black, and he simply stared at Nelly for a moment before asking her to sign the pad he'd been writing in. She looked at the pad and calmly said:

"I'm not signing that. You wrote down that I said I was going forty. I said I was going thirty-five or forty. That's not right."

"Are you refusing to cooperate?"

"No, I'm just saying…"

"Ma'am, get out of the vehicle."

Things got out of hand quickly. Nelly hesitated to move, so the policeman opened her car door, dragged her out, and slammed her face-first onto the hood while handcuffing her wrists behind her. As this was happening, the amicable cop walked quickly back from the squad car.

"What the hell happened here?"

"Exactly! Ask your partner here! He went fucking crazy on me. Are you really gonna arrest me? Are you really gonna do this?"

"Sign your statement, and you're free to go. Otherwise, you're going to the station for a while."

The amicable cop hadn't said anything other than asking what was going on. He didn't appear to be interested in stopping his partner from proceeding with his course of action, and Nelly knew she was beaten.

"Fine! Fine! I'll sign it! I don't want any trouble, and I don't know what's going on here!"

She knew she couldn't afford to be late to work. There was a new girl who seemed all nicey-nice and could use the time Nelly was gone to ingratiate herself the way Nelly had done while the woman she was covering for was away. The new girl could start making friends with the crew and remembering names and God knows what else.

Nelly thought, "I need to get the fuck out of

here." So she signed the statement, got a $100 ticket, which the mean cop cruelly reminded her she could fight in court, and headed in to work.

She spent the day telling everyone about the police incident; it briefly overshadowed the whole pants fiasco. The incident certainly got the sympathy of the men. They all cried out in disbelief: "They put their hands on you for a speeding ticket? You know you could take them to court. Get a lawyer and sue the city!"

She heard a lot of protective tirades that day, but still, there was something about the whole event and that mean cop that made her know that it was best not to mess with the situation. She had a bad feeling and a strong instinct that made her know to be scared. The paranoid intuition by which she lived told her to stand back, because she sensed that the frowning cop would be as callous and vengeful with her as she would be with a background actor who spilled cranberry juice on his costume.

Nelly felt defenseless in a way she didn't like, but she knew not to rock the boat. So her mind headed back to her pants and the dry cleaner, channeling her anger and powerless frustration into that other situation.

She got home late that night again, but once more she went and stared into the dry cleaner's window after parking her car. She read and reread their "Going Out of Business" signs and thought about what she could do next. The only thing she knew she could do was go back the next day.

Nelly slept badly. She set her alarm and reset it, worrying about oversleeping after a night of replaying the day's events in her head. She had stayed up doing more research on the Internet about police brutality and suing the city but had soon returned to the question of small claims courts and suing businesses. She imagined the vindication of watching a Judge Judy–type dressing down the dry cleaner and forcing her to right her wrongs. A public courtroom victory.

She fell asleep not too long before it was time to get up again.

When the alarm went off, she jumped up and dressed all in one uninterrupted leap. She felt confused and weird, and she was too agitated to even slow down for a few minutes to get the coffee she so badly needed.

She had dreamt about the policeman from the day before holding hands with the Asian lady, guarding her store and making Nelly move to another street. It had felt real, and she had gasped and cried with anger and what strangely enough felt like shame—an old unexplored feeling that she despised.

Nelly knew that if she slowed down too much, she would be gripped by the bizarre shame and accompanying fear that she'd woken up with, so she took the next leap out her front door and stomped over to the dry cleaner's shop. She didn't even pause outside the door or look through the glass first. She blew in, and her body carried her straight to the counter. The Asian woman saw Nelly, turned, and walked into the back of the store behind the racks.

Nelly began slamming the palm of her hand on the little desk bell over and over and suddenly had the terrible vision of the woman returning with a shotgun—no…. Impossible.

There was a flurry of plastic and movement as the dry cleaning woman came running back to the front of the store. She had something in her hand, but Nelly just kept hitting the bell, unable to stop the rhythm she had rocked herself into.

The dry cleaner stood before Nelly and held what was in her hand out to her.

She was holding a pair of dark pants hanging neatly underneath dry cleaning plastic. They were Nelly's pants—she could see the tag.

Nelly stopped slamming the bell and slowly reached up to take the item from her. She quickly lifted the plastic wrap and found the pants to be in perfect condition—clean and pressed.

Nelly's head snapped up as she heard the dry cleaning woman calmly say:

"$6.22."

Nelly paused, then reached into her purse and took out some bills and change. She didn't want to know anything about how the pants had turned up. She didn't want to argue about paying or a receipt or anything else.

She handed the woman the money and pulled the pants close to her chest.

They stared at each other briefly, and then Nelly walked out slowly, not daring to look back. Something chilled her to the bone. She knew she would never come back to the store even after it housed a different business. She would never come anywhere near the place again.

*

Nelly's fantasy was very elaborate. It had developed over a few years of real mulling over. She'd rarely taken the time to look at the basis of the fantasy and what it was about; why it felt for her like a drug that when she was ruminating and deep inside it, she derived the sort of pleasure nothing else in life gave her. It went like this: she was who she was, a costumer, and somehow she ended up working on a film in the Middle East, perhaps Turkey or somewhere not too unstable but with borders next to Iraq or some other dangerous country. And in her fantasy, she and a couple of guys from the crew—no girls, just guys, one with a camera—would go on a little trip, an exploration to buy clothes or sightsee or do something away from the rest of the crew. And they would somehow cross the bad border and get lost and captured by enemy forces.

She'd seen lots of films—all comedies—about

that sort of thing. But the difference in her fantasy was that there was someone filming it so it would become an accidental documentary, and she would immediately be the chosen leader of the three or four or however many, depending on the day of her fantasy, there were in her little expedition group.

And all sorts of things would happen. They would stumble onto a village and would have to help people. They would meet American soldiers who were evil and would somehow document their evil deeds, and with a laptop they'd send the information back to maybe the French consulate since the American consulate might not be trustworthy. They'd send it to someone who would put the footage on the web. The camera rolling and things really going down and Nelly's bravery documented for all the Prius-driving liberals in the US to see and admire.

And because her clothes were slowly getting dirty and torn, she was also getting sexier in the footage. All her knowledge of pop culture was coming out as they'd be forced to sleep outside, and she'd wake up to the sound of bombs and say something clever like, "I love the smell of napalm in the morning," and everyone would laugh at the *Apocalypse Now* reference and how funny she was. And maybe they'd still have their walkie-talkies so they'd try to communicate with each other, and she'd jokingly use a lint roller and try to get the desert dust off her ripped-up clothes as her bare legs browned in the sun.

This fantasy had grown in detail and scope. Sometimes she would be exercising, trying to lose all the crazy fat that came from nowhere, and the fantasy would be all she had left to hide in. It wasn't the events of the fantasy so much as seeing herself in the eyes of the audience—the American audience who would watch as she went to court to fight to have the documentary shown, for whatever reason. It was through the eyes of every person she had ever met that she saw herself. Going into their heads to hear their thoughts: "I never realized how amazing that girl was," or famous people saying, "My God, I would love to meet this person"—becoming the idol of famous people so that she would almost transcend fame into a whole other place. She would be a famous person's famous person.

She would think about the three-hour documentary that would then win an Oscar and how, when she would go up to receive her Oscar, she would have a limp, and everyone in the audience would know it was from the second act in the documentary where she was tortured by soldiers but would not crack and how she kicked one in the head, which made him shoot her in the leg out of rage. They would know that's what the limp was, and they would have cried at that scene, so they would cry again as they saw her victoriously go up to the stage and get her Oscar from Hugh Jackman or some other fantastically handsome man who was brought close to tears by her small thinness.

They would all stand and clap and never be the same again.

This fantasy was more real to her than anything in her life. This fantasy took her out of all the things that were happening to her in life. At times she could walk for hours and not realize that she had walked past any recognizable landscape. She could drive for miles and not feel the distance because she didn't realize what she was missing in real time. What was playing behind her eyes was actually robbing her of being alive in reality.

The fantasy seemed noble and great, and she wondered whether it was even doable. She thought of it, not as she would see it parodied in various ways, like in *Tropic Thunder* or *Three Kings*, where they got caught up in the color and satire. Her story would be real. It would have the grainy texture of a true documentary, and she would become a folk hero.

She took no steps, however, to realize this fantasy. She never looked up information about films shooting abroad. Everyone thought about working on a film, but she would always just stick to television. She never really wanted to leave her neighborhood even. She liked her local croissants and cappuccinos in the morning.

So the fantasy stayed in its own realm of fantasy. Little was done to even make it into a realistic ambition. It was self-contained, its own thing.

And the payoff of dreaming it to its limits was intoxicating in a way that perhaps the reality would not be, the elaborate images of *Maxim* magazine naming her the most interesting and therefore the sexiest woman ever, or *Esquire* the person we would marry or *GQ* the coolest chick of all time. And how women would want to be her friend and would no longer be cold towards her because they would know that she was better than them, and she would too. They would give up the competition and would simply just want to be her sidekick.

And all the men would say, "This is what I meant when I said I wanted the perfect woman," and they would love her, and she would not feel so alone anymore.

She even thought about what happened to the other characters—the person shooting her imaginary documentary or the other crew members. They would be exposed as cowards. In one scene of her fantasy, she would yell out at one of them:

"Pull yourself together! Stop crying and take pictures of those atrocities so we can show it to the world. So people will not have died for nothing."

Or, in another scene, she would lecture one of the crew about being a liberal in his cushy little fraternity world but completely useless and a coward in the field of action.

So, in the final version, she would drop everyone but the cameraman, since he was needed. And then it would be time for him to give his speech about how much he had learned from her and how she had saved his life. And in the audience would be maybe her family. Maybe the perfect man whom she had met in the editing bay—a handsome, rugged guy now holding the baby she would've had during the time between the documentary's release and Oscar night.

What Nelly wanted was fame. She wanted everything that she thought fame was. She wanted the things that she thought it promised. And one thing would dim all the other things. It would be a giant strainer that would catch all the stuff she wouldn't have to solve anymore. All the daily small problems, because they would be in one giant, Fannie Mae–like consolidation loan: fame.

She would not have to deal with intimacy or friendship. It would be unnecessary. There would be thousands upon thousands of people who would already love her. She would not have to earn any sort of love. She would not have to relate within relationships. One half of the relating would already be done, and very little would be expected of her. She would simply just have to *be* and let everyone work around her.

The ultimate life—everything she did was in order for her to somehow come closer to seeing herself through the lens of fame, through the lens of being loved without having to be lovable—at least in person.

She wanted to be an object. She wanted to be objectified. This is why she'd been drawn to the writer. She had, even while with him, seen the whole story as something written up in *Vanity Fair*, a grand love story where someone would be narrating and describing her, her hair or her skin and what she had meant to the writer. She wanted to know what people thought of her without actually being aware of what she was. Fame was the only way out of the task of actually living her life and dealing with all the human intimacy that would be required for that life to become worthwhile and real.

*

Los Angeles was probably just about the worst place where a teenage Nelly could've grown up in the '80s and '90s.

Although she was in her twenties during the '90s, it was as if her teenage angst never quite went away. It lingered into post-pubescence and well into her thirties. Still, it was truly her teens when the imprints of all her complexes were made. Growing up in Beverly Hills and being surrounded by wealth and fame and yet not having any access to it pretty much drove Nelly crazy.

Her parents had a rented one-bedroom apartment. They were tailors and did all their alterations from home. At night they went to their bedroom and slept while Nelly got the living room as her bedroom. It was funny that she grew up that way and then went on into the workforce, where people assumed that Nelly was a rich kid. But she hadn't even had her own bedroom, and she had no qualms about letting people know this.

Her parents had had money at some point, she knew, in whatever Mediterranean hellhole her father was from, but by the time she came around it was all gone.

She went to Beverly Hills High School and sat next to people like A-list actors' and producers' daughters or whoever else, while she, herself, was an anonymous nobody, and she knew it.

By the time she was fifteen or sixteen, she was going to all kinds of clubs with her fake ID. She and Bill would tear around, going to places like Flaming Colossus in downtown LA, an incredible warehouse club on Bonnie Brae where you would step into what seemed on the outside like a dirty little dive bar but turned out to be a huge, tented, magnificent exotic palace filled with fire-eaters, spiral staircases, zinc bars, and everything else that you might have imagined in a fantastic dream, including having Bono and Mickey Rourke drinking side by side and smiling at teenaged Nelly as if she was attractive and famous.

So these underground places, these hidden things, kept her going, and Bill would come along for the ride. Nelly would somehow hear about these places, and she would need help to get there. It was

Bill who got them their fake IDs. It was Bill who would always drive. But it was Nelly who was the brains behind the operation. She was the one who'd know that they had to go to Sixth and Alameda, where men would be standing on the corner with a handful of flyers telling them the address to where the real party was, and they would say mysteriously, "All the fun you need, all the fun indeed," quoting *Dr. Seuss on the Loose* or some shit like that.

Once they would get to the party, the warehouse would be decrepit, the party throwers having broken into the condemned location to set the place up. The Dr. Seuss theme would become warped, and the baldheaded go-go dancers with no pants on had some weird stripy hat things on their heads to let you know that perhaps they were alluding to a children's book. Then it would turn into a strange nightmare where giant papier-mâché penises would spew dry ice in the middle of the dance floor, and people would be falling down doing God knows what right on the floor, and the children's book similarities would end quickly.

But still it was amazing and different, and none of the Beverly Hills High School idiots knew anything about it. It was more a Fairfax High and Hollywood High kind of scene—those were the cool kids; they knew what it was about.

But still Nelly never felt a part of it all and never understood that most other teens didn't, either. Not in the little coffee shop called The Living Room—the very first place she ever saw people sitting on couches and playing chess or backgammon, or reading books while having their coffee. She never even felt a part of Café Pick Me Up, where all the freaks would go, where everybody fit in because nobody fit in, and people would sprinkle meth in your coffee as a gesture of friendship. She never felt right in King King on Third Street or Power Tools—a club so big and so loud you could be anyone you wanted to be—right enough to fit in, anyway.

But Nelly fit in nowhere. Nowhere. She would find herself dancing somewhere—maybe at Plastic Passion—and she'd turn to the side and see the teenaged Drew Barrymore dancing next to her, and she would be filled with shame. She would see how tiny Drew was, how short and petite with her lineage of famous ancestors, and Nelly knew she could never be LA royalty, and she would want to die.

She hated the rich and famous people, but she also hated the hipsters who'd go downtown to Gorky's to eat potato knishes after a night of dancing—the UCLA English majors who were oh-so-clever and didn't care about fame or money but dealt in the currency of cool. She wasn't cool enough either, and she didn't have what it took. They saw her as a future sorority girl who would end up in a UC but not a cool one like UCLA—one of the faraway, last-choice UCs.

She never dyed her hair either—it was always straight and shiny. Nor did she wear a lot of makeup.

She just didn't look right, and whenever she bought clothes, she bought expensive, "classy" items, something about them or maybe the way she wore them making them look like they were from Kmart. The clothes made her look like an older mom, even in her teens.

This deep awkwardness in the city where everyone was carrying their stereos around like lunch boxes, where MTV was king and girls' wrists were laden with black rubber bracelets, and there were places like Poo-na-na Sook, where you could go upstairs and hang around with Pauly Shore or come downstairs and have impossibly thin french fries.

The whole place was one giant playground—all you needed was a car and an attitude. And even that light, absurd fun was squashed by her deep, deep hatred.

Still, to Bill, she was heroic—she was a mover and shaker in getting things done. As far as Bill could tell, she was cool, and she was rich, and she was famous. In Bill's eyes, she was a star. And he knew that it was all like one big John Hughes movie where he was Duckie and she was Molly Ringwald, and she was always looking for that Andrew McCarthy type or the evil James Spader type. Some other boy, a boy that was not Duckie, not Jon Cryer. She wanted the Judd Nelson or the God knows who else—Emilio Estevez—the boy who would come in and finally make her right.

The boy who would come and give her her rightful crown.

Bill felt that that's what she was looking for when they went out. She was not looking for a good time. She wasn't looking to dance and have fun and listen to the music. She wasn't looking to laugh or just be fulfilled or talk about the future. She was simply out there looking for someone to discover and rescue her. She was out because she knew that if there was a prince, he wouldn't find her in her parents' one bedroom, sitting on the couch. She was out to let herself be seen by whoever it was that was going to take her out of her own life and install her in the life she thought she deserved—the one she was not living.

And once in a while, a guy would come along, and Bill would feel the discomfort and cold breeze of the unspoken: Nelly wanted him to step back while she talked to the loser. And she would talk to the guy for a while and maybe exchange numbers. Some of it would be magical, and then she would talk about the guy all the way home, and some of it wouldn't be so magical, like the guy she though was from Prague and he was twenty-six, which made him exotic instead of old. He had taken her to Formosa Café, and during their date he looked out the window and watched a woman walk by, and said, "Isn't she beautiful? Why are women so much more beautiful than men?" Then he looked back at Nelly and said, "You know, your nose is very interesting."

Nelly got up and left at that point—luckily she was sixteen and, having borrowed Bill's beat-up old Dodge Dart, was able to get herself back home and tell Bill that he could come get his car. Bill would get a ride from his older brother and come over to get his car from Nelly and suffer the questions from his brother on the way there: "Why are you such a pussy? You know she's fucking you over? You know that she's using you? Why would you give her your car to go out with some other guy? What the fuck is wrong with you, dude?"

The prince Nelly waited for never quite came. It was debatable whether there were any princes where they hung out. In the parlors and bars, there couldn't have been any princes, and if there were any they didn't look the way Nelly wanted them to, so she didn't notice them. Bill could have been her Prince Hal if she had looked. All kinds of different nerds could have been her prince on late nights at Canter's Deli—funny guys, silly guys, clever guys—the ones with the imperfect frizzy hair and not quite tall enough and not quite buff enough.

But Nelly wanted to marry up and out. She didn't want her own male equivalent, and that was the whole tragedy of it. She starved her own personality and her own charm and her joie de vivre to fit a guy who didn't exist.

The spark that had to exist in order to fall in love—that was all squashed away because of her single-minded determination and hard focus on getting something that she thought she wanted. It took the fun out of her, and so she became unknowable, hardened, and childlike in her inability to accept reality. She got older, but her teenage obsessions were not just passing things.

Bill still loved her, but as the years went by, she became more and more hard and determined. Looking for the thing that would save her began to calcify her personality. She filled up with a sense of entitlement and disappointment, until she was angry and forgot what it was that she wanted in the first place, forgot what it was that she wanted to be saved from through fame or money by the Prince. She forgot that she was simply hurt that she had to sleep on the couch while her parents got the bedroom. She was hurt that she didn't have a car while the other kids did and her parents insisted on living in a place where there was all this wealth she never got to touch. She was hurt that she had a receding chin and that her mother thought she wasn't pretty enough, and she was hurt that her father was always preoccupied and in his own head. She did not feel good enough. It was that simple. It was that no one had ever taken care of her except Bill. And she abused Bill.

And the princes would come and go and come and go, and none of them would stick because none of them would see a girl who was lovable and vulnerable way down deep underneath the hard shell of the woman who demanded things from them.

*

Nelly had tried everything, and finally she was going to do what all the fat girls did—go to Weight Watchers.

She woke up each day, and she could feel the difference in her body, and it would just bring her to tears. She would run her hands down the front and sides of her body past what used to be her rib cage, down the sides of what used to be her hollow belly over to what used to be her hip bones and her narrow side. What she found instead was a lumpy terrain of unfamiliarity.

She could not understand it. She had gone and had her thyroid checked again, and they had found nothing. They had suggested that she try aromatherapy and acupuncture, and finally they suggested Weight Watchers—something that horrified her and made her think that they did not understand that she was simply a thin person who had accidentally been captured in the body of a fat person, and that all they had to do was find the correct password back to her normal shape so she would be fine.

The doctors looked at her as if she was a real fat person—as if she had really done this to herself or that she had been born this way. She started taking them photos of herself—of her real self—to show them. "Look, look," she would say, "this is who I know I am.

Somehow there's been a mix-up, and I've accidentally gotten caught in this body and need my real body back right now. I will take a pill and do whatever it takes— get some shots? Maybe surgery? I don't care."

What she did not want to hear was the thing that horrified her when they casually uttered it: "Have you tried going on a diet and upping your exercise?" This is when her face would fall because they were talking to her like she was really fat, like this was her real self, and so she had to do what all fat people had to do and refused to do it, which was to diet or run around the track or go to a gym and run around there and sweat with the other fat people who parade around in stretch pants. They treated her like she was really one of those people.

She walked out of the doctor's office or more like waddled out. Her arms and legs were chafing so badly that she could not go out without wearing strangely soft baby-like clothing—light cotton pants supposedly for exercise, but she doubted anyone who was that big would be doing any yoga or anything else other than sitting on their couch and eating entire rotisserie chickens every few minutes.

The thing was that now she wasn't even really eating—she was not eating anything highly caloric, anyway. She would have some lettuce when she was a little hungry but would not eat anything else, so there wasn't even any chance that what was happening to her body was some miscalculation of calories. There weren't any calories going in, *nothing*—and this wasn't hard for her, having been an anorexic at one point. She knew how to starve herself, knew how much to eat to survive but not gain weight, knew how to run her ass ragged to lose five pounds in three days, and that's what she was doing. She was running around and starving herself, but nothing was happening. She was on a hard-core anorexic's diet.

Fat people don't have that discipline. Fat people need their food. They need little tastes of this and little tastes of that, and they need a nibble of chocolate and a little bit of pizza or fake, small portions of all those things, or they'll go fucking crazy from not eating.

All she needed was a leaf of lettuce. And that's all she had.

She used to walk by the little Weight Watchers store at the mall where they had candies and treats and frozen crap that people could eat, and boy was that crap supposed to be just as good as the real thing. The fatties congregated in there, just munching on that stuff and thinking that if one of the candies tasted good, then two would taste better, and if it was low-fat, they couldn't get fat. So they'd throw their money on the counter, and Weight Watchers would just rake in crazy cash off these people.

But Nelly refused to be one of them. She wasn't one of them, and she wasn't going to go in there and even entertain the idea of a healthy balanced diet and exercise as if somehow she didn't know what being skinny was about and what it took. She *was* skinny. This was some sort of hormonal pituitary nightmare, and she was going to find a doctor who could figure it out. If it wasn't a Western doctor, it was going to be an Eastern doctor who was going to make up some sort of shitty tea for her to drink and stick needles in her ass. Either way, it had to be fixed.

*

Back at work, she was getting treated differently. Whenever she went around the craft service table, or there was a catered lunch, people wanted to see what exactly she was eating, what exactly it was that she was doing to make herself so huge.

This was not just her imagination. It really was what they were thinking. The hair and makeup girls talked about it quite a bit. It was the best thing to come up for the gossip mill in ages. They just couldn't believe it: she was massive, and she got that way in a matter of weeks. It was like she gained seven or eight dress sizes—it was bizarre, like she was just somebody else.

And Nelly knew what the deal was with the gossip and spent most of her day telling people about how it was a pituitary or thyroid issue. That it totally acted up, and the doctors hadn't figured out how to reverse it, but they would.

One of the actresses heard this and decided to tell her about her acupuncturist, but even while trying to help Nelly solve her problem they all secretly enjoyed believing and knowing in their hearts and picturing her stuffing Twinkies into her face. Getting up in the middle of the night, opening her well-stocked fridge, sitting down on the floor, and just starting to chow down. And they all started looking at what she was eating off the craft service table, so that they could avoid that food.

Her fatness made the fat girls feel better—there were a few of them in the office usually, the production coordinator and a couple of the other girls who did manly jobs. There was one girl grip you'd call husky and those girl PAs who thought of their fatness as tomboyish. They thought of themselves as not being froufrou girly girls and took pride in being more like boys. So they thought it was okay that they were a little chubbier and had a muffin top hanging over their jeans. They thought it was cute, and it was to some; their seemingly baby-like fat made them young and attractive to the older, weirder men.

But the sort of fat that Nelly was getting or had gotten and was continuing to get was a different kind of fat. It was like older sedentary lady fat. Las Vegas fat. Nubby, velveteen, burgundy-sweat-suit kind of fat. It was the fat of advanced age found in men living in the sticks.

It made her hair seem fat even though she still tried to wear it straight. Young stringy skinny hair was her usual style, but something about her hair got unruly and out of control. Maybe it was because she couldn't get her arms far back enough to do a smooth ponytail. But it seemed like it was a thicker ponytail somehow, and the elastic band would not go around all the way.

*

The letters were the longest and most astonishing documents that she had ever seen in her life, and she could not believe that they were written to her, for her, or were in any way inspired by her existence. It took her a while to think of them as letters.

She liked the idea of the letters more than the actual letters themselves. She read them only once, but she did know that anyone else, especially someone who may have been a fan of the writer's, would probably have pored over the documents and read them over and over again. The fact that they had footnotes and subcategories and subject headings somehow made it seem like the letters were not about her, though they did contain detailed responses to every word she had written to him in her letters.

The thoroughness of his answers did not change the fact that somewhere deep down inside, she got the distinct feeling that the writer didn't really care who it was that he was writing to. She felt that he just wanted to see himself write, in the way that some people wanted to hear themselves speak. But still, she was flattered and showed her friends the letters from a certain distance—very old friends she hadn't seen in some time, uninvolved with her enough that she could imagine them to be trusted friends.

Anyway, she put the letters away and always thought, "You know, someday those can be very valuable documents. Very valuable American documents." The writer was an important member of her generation's literary world, and no one could dispute that.

Later, when the affair did start to sour, she thought to herself, "I could really fuck him up with these letters…. I could just send them somewhere and have them printed, and people would know that he cheated with me—he cheated on his girlfriend or whatever she was. I can't believe he sent all this stuff, and you know it's clearly him, it's his style, and he signed it in pen and did his weird little swivel that everyone recognizes. The little stick men that he does all the time. I could really fucking hurt him."

But she put the letters away and didn't think much about them, quickly obsessing over something else instead. She knew that somebody like him was protected, and if she were to try and expose the letters with malice, not only would they alert him but they would keep the letters, throw them away somehow or give them back to him. Plus she would be branded a lunatic. It would be clear that she really just wanted people to recognize her for her association with him, and she would be ridiculed.

So the time did not seem right. There was really nothing she could do except just gloat quietly about having letters from him. Once in a while she'd meet somebody who knew him or was in his inner circle, and she'd find some way to hint at her association, but she never dared do more.

But all that changed on the day he killed himself. She realized that finally, if she were to make the letters known to the public, he wouldn't be there to argue or dispute that he broke it off with her and that none of it had meant a thing. They would be her incredible documents from him, which would just surface—his thoughtful languishing notes would be seen as love letters to a woman he had cared about. They would know nothing of how the affair ended or who ended it.

No one could argue that it was important for these documents to be seen, now that he was dead. And she would become famous. They would be the famous letters with her name attached, and there would be more things for people to read written by him.

There was no way anyone could vilify her, and there was no way that she could look bad. Even the woman that he was with before his death was not the one he had been with when she knew him and whom he'd been cheating on, so even that was not a problem—even the adultery was past and gone and forgotten.

She spent only a brief moment or two thinking about his death, about what he might have been going through, or if she remembered that he was even the sort of man who was prone to sadness. She thought about him in his last hour on earth for all of thirty seconds. She stopped to wonder if he really intended to die. Ultimately, she found that her feelings of annoyance with him still outweighed any human pity that anyone else might have felt for him and certainly outweighed any sort of idol worship.

She knew that she had to figure out which publication to send the letters to, but there was no rush. She kept the notes in a box in the trunk of her newly leased BMW, which she had to get sooner than planned in order to distract herself from the onslaught of hostile fat. This way, the letters were always nearby and secure. More secure than they would have been in her apartment.

She decided that maybe she could talk to Bill about this. His girlfriend was a bookstore egghead, and she might know who would be a good person to go to. The letters and certainly who they were from would surely get some money. Yes, a little bit of clever fame mixed together with a little bit of money, and throw in the historical relevance—you can't get any better than that, Nelly thought.

For about a week or so, every time public radio came on in any car or at home, all anyone could hear was the radio host—what's his name—droning and whining about the dead writer in between pledge drives and groveling for money. But soon all the tributes and memorials tapered off. Nelly thought that perhaps she should strike while the iron was hot, but she realized that these types of bookish people had a sense of decency, especially about death, and especially about how much time should pass before dancing on graves, et cetera, so she thought she'd sit on the letters for a little bit.

But she thought of what could happen and how the whole thing would blow up a new storm of talk—talk about love letters, maybe even in *Vanity Fair*, maybe she could skip *Harper's*, maybe she could skip the brainy magazines and go straight to *Vanity Fair*, and they'd print a picture of how beautiful she was and why he would be so driven to write to her—these thoughts made her nuts with images of outfits and orange Hermès boxes. She would think about that day, and it would make her happy. And she felt that at last something made sense.

This was how it was to happen, and thus the complete inconvenience and insult of the man dumping her and pulling away was finally justified.

*

Nelly waddled across the parking lot after parking her car and headed up to the entrance of the building on Los Robles in Pasadena. Luckily, the office was on the first floor, since even taking the elevator anywhere was too much of a hardship for Nelly at this point. She didn't even really walk forward but went from side to side and then teetered forward, in some way using gravity to propel her in the direction she needed to go.

She walked into the open office, and an electronic bell went off. She must have tripped a sensor that was placed there to let the person know that someone was in the waiting room. She looked at the chairs and realized immediately that they had handles, meaning that she would not be able to get herself into them, she was far wider than that—so she stood sweating and close to tears. She walked over to the credenza in the small waiting room and saw that there were typed-up testimonials by various patients who had come through the office and seen the doctors. Testimonials saying that their back pain or their PMS had gone away. Infertile women saying that they'd been popping out babies ever since the good doctor had jammed a few needles into their ovaries.

There was no mention of weight loss, and this did not make Nelly happy. Next to the testimonials there was a bowl of chocolate kisses. She just sneered at them—she didn't want chocolate kisses. She didn't want candy or food, and that was the part that annoyed her the most. People assumed that she was enjoying a little gluttony-fest when she really wasn't. She still wasn't a foodie, never had been, never would be. She was a picky eater. She liked sprouts, macrobiotic crap, and tofu. Healthy food that tasted too awful to gorge on.

She stood for a while and then started to figure out where the motion detector was, since she accidentally tripped it by changing weight from one leg to the other, and then she began to do it on purpose, over and over again, until finally the doctor came scurrying out.

The doctor wore great big glasses that made her eyes huge, her hair was in a sort of sprayed-up helmet, and her teeth were not very good, so Nelly was immediately discouraged. Her English was even worse, and suddenly Nelly felt like she was having a flashback to her whole problem at the dry cleaner, but she tried to put that out of her mind.

The doctor tried to ask her questions about what the problem was and may or may not have understood the answer. She led Nelly into the other room and told her to lie down on the table with the disposable paper and tiny pillow that looked like it had been stolen from an airline. Nelly just sat there for a moment while the acupuncturist looked at her and said: "You are fat! We make you better!"

Nelly was glad the woman understood that she was fat. The word certainly didn't offend her, because she did not identify with the fat population or find it offensive if somebody called her fat instead of husky or a little overweight. Instead, Nelly's heart filled with hope. She lay down on the table and pulled her arms in next to her sides as best she could, since there was very little room on the table for her arms once her whole body had widened and spread out.

The doctor put on some music—some of that strange but familiar department store music—and it was indeed very relaxing, especially in conjunction with the heat lamp that was pointed directly at Nelly's head. The doctor took out some alcohol swabs and rubbed the top of Nelly's head, then took a needle like the kind used in sewing machines and put it in the middle of Nelly's forehead, banging it ever so slightly into the flesh. Tap, tap, tap.

The doctor walked out, leaving her alone in the room after flipping off the light. When Nelly closed her eyes, she saw blue explosions of color behind her eyelids. She saw neon and electric bolts of lightning, and she wondered if this was normal. The heat lamp was heating up the needle in her head, and suddenly she wondered what it was that she was feeling in that moment. She took a deep breath and realized that perhaps it was peace. She felt a profound sense of nothingness. There was no worry in her head, and she felt a deep need to know what this was all about.

She went in and out of sleep in a strange meditative fantasy state, and before she knew it, the doctor had come back to pull out the needles and send her on her merry way, knowing that her insurance would fully cover the plan.

She didn't know what had happened or what the

needles were for or what they were addressing, only that she would be back the next day for more. She didn't believe it would ever work, but something about the explosions of blue light behind her eyes, something about the pain followed by calm, made her want to come back.

Having never done drugs, having always been too much of a control freak for something like that, what Nelly didn't realize was that what she had experienced was the bliss that one could access with many drugs—for at least the first few times. The euphoria came from certain neurotransmitters being fired up. It was her own brain chemistry, which usually tended towards hyper freak-out mode, that had given her the bliss. So this was new, calm, and amazing, and it had the potential for an addictive reaction from somebody like Nelly, whose whole life was brittle and crispy.

Nelly came back the next day, and the doctor said a lot less this time, simply looked at her when she arrived. Nelly heard her on the telephone talking furiously in a foreign language she couldn't recognize in that way that made it sound like there was a fight even when there wasn't. The German language sometimes gave that impression. It was very upsetting and disconcerting, and it made the gentle speakers of French and English uncomfortable.

Nelly had imagined that she lost weight the night before. She wasn't sure whether she had or not, because she could not get on the scale any longer since she'd broken it, and then, having replaced it, she broke the second one too. But she felt thinner as she lay on the table in anticipation, hoping that it would be the same feeling and that if she did this enough times, she would get back to normal. She waited while the doctor went around her body and jammed her with needles. She still put the ones in her head but added more to the tops of her hands and feet. She stuck needles into her belly after pulling up her giant shirt and looking at the rolls of fat. Nelly thought she could feel the pain vibrating through every nerve ending and bouncing off like a pinball all over her body. She cried out in anger, then something strange that the anger was covering.

The doctor said: "It's good, it's good—let out anger."

The doctor this time put the heat lamp on her belly, and when she flipped on the light Nelly saw small electric explosions of lava—volcanic fire pouring behind her eyelids with black underneath, and then the whole thing switched to a forest green. Then it all went to black.

It seemed like the doctor had been gone for forty-five minutes when she came back and slowly began to take out the needles. Nelly didn't want her to stop, so she made an appointment for the next day, and this is how it went on and on, with Nelly imagining she was losing weight. By the fifth day, it appeared that she really *was* losing weight because she was wearing black, which was encouraging. Nelly knew that even if she wasn't, there was some answer in that room for her—something familiar, something she was on the verge of finding out, so she would not give up on it yet.

By the third week, the doctor with the needles had stuck her so many times that Nelly didn't pay attention anymore. The table felt like it was so much roomier: Nelly would spread out and be able to spread her legs a little bit, and since slimming down her middle part there was more room for her arms to lie with her palms facing up towards the ceiling.

She was excited and preoccupied—somewhat addicted to the sensation of the acupuncture—and so she would come in and not pay much attention to the doctor and her mumblings. She didn't notice that more and more she was speaking in that layered foreign language to herself while she was around Nelly. The doctor would look her up and down and make her stick out her tongue, then look in her eyes and shake her finger at Nelly's face once in a while and say something inaudible.

It was a Tuesday in November, and Nelly was on her way to vote in the presidential election. She decided that she would go to acupuncture before voting, so she could decide things with a clearer head afterward, since she had not made up her mind whom to vote for. She arrived as usual, no longer waddling but almost skipping. She was now just slightly heavy.

People at work had already forgotten about the extreme and crazy way her weight had gone up. As she had begun to normalize, they forgot about the drama of it all.

They forgot about her crying, they forgot about the whole issue of her pants being lost by the dry cleaner or being pulled over by cops or any of the other things that had bothered her that she would report to the people she worked with.

They were not real friendships at the job, so people were able to hear one another's stories and then quickly empty the files and vacate the space for new information. Being a freelance mercenary kind of world, there was no particular attachment to any one person, and so nobody really noticed more than they needed to at any given time, and people forgot quickly. Very quickly.

Nelly skipped into the office and walked right into the room where she was supposed to lie down, bypassing the waiting room altogether, hearing the bing-bong at the door as she walked past and wondering if the bell made less noise because she was lighter now, but probably not since it was only a motion sensor, not a fat-ass sensor.

She lay down on the crunchy paper covering the table, and the doctor came in and looked at her, cocked her head a little bit, and said, "Yes, yes, yes."

Nelly prepared herself and even grew a little impatient, waiting for the bliss, for the nirvana she wanted to blaze out inside her. She didn't want to feel any discomfort ever again. She had become a big advocate of Eastern medicine or whatever it was that numbed her pain. She thought she could do this forever. If it was good for her and make her feel good, why not?

She realized after looking on the Internet that there was supposed be some greater understanding of what she was feeling through this Eastern medicine, that there was an underlying moral story to everything and a lifestyle that went with the whole deal. That bliss was not, in fact, the objective but just a byproduct of living this way. But Nelly didn't care about all that. She just liked the bliss.

The doctor walked in and told her to put her palms up towards the ceiling, the backs of her hands flat on the table, and her feet relaxed and spread slightly apart.

The doctor slowly went about doing what she usually did, putting alcohol on Nelly's skin with a swab, then sticking one needle into her forehead. She had never put a needle in the palms of Nelly's hands before, so she really wasn't expecting to feel the wetness of the alcohol rub, which made her fingers move slightly. She felt the tip of the needle in the middle of one hand, followed by a slight pinch.

She braced herself, but what she felt was like nothing she had ever imagined. It was as if a hammer had come down on a giant nail and gone right through her hand. She thought she heard an explosion, and she saw lights behind her eyes, fireworks, and a white light.

She could not move her body. She thought she had screamed, but she could not hear her own voice. She felt the tip of the needle on her other hand and struggled to move to avoid the next pounding, but it happened too quickly, and she even thought she heard metal on metal followed by a bang as the hammer hit the needle and jammed it through her hand.

Her eyes were closed—she could not open them to look at what was going on around her. She felt the coldness on the tops of her feet, and suddenly the same huge pounding nail through each foot. She thought she was going to scream again—she thought she was going to die. But no noise would come out of her.

She was drenched—sweat dripped down her body. She heard as if from a long, long distance the doctor walking out the door and flipping off the light.

This time, behind her eyes, Nelly saw explosions of white sky-blue. It was as if she had been shot out of a cannon into the sky and then was floating and probably falling downwards, but very slowly. She was free floating, and it was terrifying and beautiful.

Her hands and feet throbbed with enormous pain, and she thought she felt the wetness of blood dripping all around her. She didn't know what was happening nor what the purpose of this was, but it did not feel like acupuncture. It felt real. It felt like she had been injured, and it felt like she had been catapulted into the sky and was now coming down, perhaps even picking up speed bit by bit, hurtling towards the earth again.

But really she was just lying there. She wasn't doing much else.

She was experiencing crucifixion, and it was real to her. She even began to whisper prayers, and had someone been there in the room with her—someone who understood Aramaic—they would have known that she was more than just a patient who was there to lose weight through acupuncture. She was more than a vain woman on a surgical bed with a couple of tiny, tiny needles stuck into her hands, feet, and head. She was Christ.

CPSIA information can be obtained
at www.ICGtesting.com
Printed in the USA
FSHW011238290919
62498FS